Pure Lust

By Cassie Wild and M.S. Parker

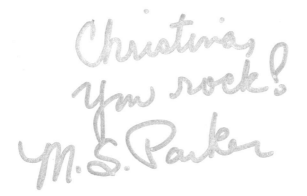

D1739230

ISBN-13: 978-1514857823

ISBN-10: 1514857820

Table of Contents

Chapter One

Three steps into the white marble and glass lobby of the Bouvier building and I knew I was so out of my league. The skyscraper housed the largest fashion house in Manhattan and there I was, a tiny little country mouse, dressed in last year's fashions.

Appointment or not, I didn't belong here. The suited man behind the counter must have thought so too. I only had a few seconds inside the bright elegance of the lobby before he addressed me coolly, "All visitors must sign in. Name?"

"Gabriella Baine."

The few people milling about a large square of white leather couches in the cavernous lobby looked up at the sound of my voice. Had I really spoken that loud?

Two bored models sipped sparkling water while a man in a close-fitting, tailored suit strode over to the windows, looking outside, then glared at his watch. The fourth person, a young man with a bright purple shirt glowing from underneath his conservative suit studied me from under his lashes, the look on his face caught between boredom and hostility.

He was wearing the same silver visitor's pin the security guard handed to me. Was he here interviewing for the same job? Bouvier, the internationally known high-end fashion house, was looking for a new talent acquisitions assistant. I guess they could have been interviewing for several positions. I tried a polite smile as I moved to sit down in the sitting area.

The man in the bright purple shirt all but growled at me.

I'm in way over my head...

"Thanks, Kendra." I muttered.

My roommate, native New Yorker and six feet of jaw-dropping natural beauty, was a model and while she hadn't quite hit the big times—*yet*—she had a few connections. She'd set up this interview as if I was a shoe-in.

As if.

Speaking of shoes, I looked down at my patent leather heels. The sexy peekaboos had plenty of shine, but they weren't designer shoes, and I was sure the people in the lobby had already noticed. Even the guy who'd opened the door for me had worn hand-cobbled loafers.

I took a deep breath and put on a fake pair of tortoise shell glasses. The stage fright trick I'd picked up studying improvisational theater in college was now a habit, though I liked to think of it more as a quirk.

It reminded me that what I really wanted out of

life was to sit in a small room surrounded by other writers, arguing out the beats, hooks, and jokes of a new television show. Not trying to sell myself as being some sort of expert in acquiring new talent.

Wearing the glasses, I could make myself look at everything as possible fodder for my writing. This would be a typical fish-out-of-water scene. Maybe I could make it different—the heroine would bolt before it was too late. Take off running down the sidewalk in a fit of hysterical panic. Crash into Prince Charming.

I could use a Prince Charming, as well as a job.

Resisting the urge to huff out a dramatic sigh, I swept the room with another nervous glance. I should bolt, though, Prince Charming or not. But I needed the job. My current job was all about connections and experience, but the pay sucked and I *needed* the money.

"Ms. Baine?"

Too late to run now. I made myself smile as I stood.

It was time to teeter across a slick white marble minefield of possible embarrassments to interview for a job I knew nothing about. *You're paying your dues*, I told myself. We all had to pay them. Kendra had paid hers and she was almost there. I had to pay mine.

"Gabriella?"

"That's, ah, me." I stumbled and tried to play it off as a quick dance shuffle in the doorway of what looked like a break room. The fake glasses slid down my nose and I hurriedly took them off. They might work to calm me, but I didn't want to explain to people why I didn't wear them all the time. That would *really* convince people I had a few screws loose.

He stepped aside, allowing me to enter. I edged in through the doorway, looking around nervously.

It was indeed a break room.

"I'm Simon Hughes." He spoke in a brisk, borderline rude voice as he came around the table and sat down. He held a file in his hand and he flipped it open, gesturing for me to sit.

I did, watching as he skimmed the information in the file.

"It says here you're from Tennessee."

"Yes." I smiled.

"I don't hear much of an accent."

I was used to this by now. It had seemed obnoxious when I'd first moved here, but one thing I'd learned early on was that the slow twang of the south wasn't going to open any doors in New York— and it might in fact slam them in my face.

"I've been gone from home a while. The accent only comes out when I'm riled." I winked, trying to lighten the tension.

The young man with the thinning blond hair just studied me with the same cool expression for a long moment. Absently, he smoothed down a skinny tie, brushed invisible lint off his tan suit and adjusted his cufflinks. Something about those gestures seemed familiar, like the way I wore my glasses. A ritual. *Possible personality quirk,* I told myself. I had an entire mental file of them.

"I'm sorry for the location," he said, glancing back down at the file. "Bouvier is having a big launch meeting upstairs and the other conference room is covered in catalog work, but at least there's coffee."

He gestured toward the counter along the wall in what I assumed was an offer. "No, thank you."

I was jittery enough.

He flipped through my application, the silence straining on my nerves until I found myself measuring the steps between me and the door, then *that* door and the main doors. Could I make a break for it in these heels?

"So, Ms. Baine." He reshuffled the papers in front of them, neatly stacked them, aligning the edges in a way that struck me as borderline obsessive. Then he did the tie, lint, cufflink check again.

The dude had enough quirks going on for a whole cast of characters all by himself.

Abruptly, he jerked his head up and pinned me with a hard look.

"Exactly what do you bring to the world of talent acquisition?"

"A need for talent?" I flashed him a smile.

"I'll rephrase." He tapped a finger on the thin file. "What is your experience in the talent industry, Ms. Baine?"

Aw, hell...

The horrible interview continued to go downhill

from there. When the door flew open nearly fifteen minutes in—had it *only* been fifteen minutes—I could have cried in relief.

Then I caught a look of the intruder.

Oh. Wow.

A jaw-dropping gorgeous intruder. He swept aside a pile of files so neatly organized, I knew they had to have been Simon Hughes' handy work and I watched as the man across from me went red in the face.

Then I slid the sexy storm another covert look. He was flinging open cabinets and grumbling. Then finally, he grunted, grabbing something from one of them, slamming the door with a resounding *bang*. He had a fistful of sugar packets.

He turned, studying us as he ripped them all open at once. Sugar spilled across the counter, only half of it going into the cup.

Simon Hughes clenched his jaw and focused on me. "I'm sorry. Please continue."

I guess we were going to pretend we were still alone.

"Aren't you Lee's assistant?" The man who wasn't supposed to be there grabbed a stirring stick as he spoke. "What are you doing on the main floor? Isn't there some kind of attic all you assistants hang in like bats?"

I laughed out loud and then had to pretend it was my ring tone. I made a good show of turning the phone off and apologizing to Simon. If he hadn't been glaring at the coffee-swilling, sugar-slinging intruder, I don't think it would have worked. As it was, neither one even glanced at me.

"I'm conducting an interview, Mr. McCreary," Simon said stiffly.

"And you haven't even introduced us. I'm Flynn." The man turned cadet blue eyes on me. All the nerves jittering inside me seemed to coalesce and then explode, turning into something else entirely. Lust.

Plain and simple.

Those blue eyes drifted down, lingered on my mouth, then back up.

Heat suffused me and I managed, barely, not to lick my lips.

He was bossy and overconfident. I knew his type. He'd be flippant and arrogant through and through. He loomed over that snotty Simon Hughes just because he could and I almost felt bad for the poor guy conducting my lousy interview. But I still had a feeling if he decided to turn his ire my way, I'd be a molten mess.

Simon shifted nervously in his chair, clearing his throat as he started his tie, lint, cufflink check. "Mr. McCreary—"

"I'm here for a job interview," I said, hoping to salvage the situation. "We've only got a set amount of time, Mr. McCreary."

He cocked an eyebrow at me before he leaned over Simon to read the top file. "Gabriella Baine, from Tennessee." He cocked an eyebrow. "Too bad you lost the accent. Accents are sexy."

I pressed my palms down on the table and spread my fingers to stop from balling my hands into fists. I didn't find that eyebrow thing sexy. Nope. And I hated that he was flirting during an interview. Definitely.

Flynn's blue eyes lingered on me, a faint smile curling his mouth. It was a beautiful mouth, just full enough without being too much. One hundred percent kissable lips.

Simon looked like he wanted to disappear into the chair, or maybe turn into the invisible lint he was now fussing with.

This was getting out of control. Aggravated, I looked back at Simon. "I'm sorry, what was your question?"

Simon went to respond, but Flynn cut him off. "Lee's assistant, a word please. In private."

Flynn yanked Simon from his chair and hauled him out the glass door. I watched as Flynn gave clear instructions with a lot of cutting hand gestures and some head shaking. Somehow I'd lost the job in a matter of syllables and I didn't know why.

As he marched away, I could see one other thing. Flynn McCreary had a great ass. Which I supposed was fitting since he *was* an ass.

The interviewer's face was flushed as he came back into the room. "Ms. Baine? Our time is up. I'll call if we have any further questions."

Why am I not surprised? "Thank you."

This entire thing had been a disaster from moment one. Without bothering to say anything

8

else, I pushed through the door. Standing in the lobby with its sparkling glass and elegant marble, I tipped my head back and stared up.

I didn't belong here and I wasn't going to pretend like I did.

Kicking off the borrowed heels, I picked them up and walked barefoot across the lobby. Just before I reached the door, the skin on the back of my neck prickled. Swinging my head around, I caught sight of the bastard who'd cut my interview short.

Flynn McCreary stood at the visitor's desk and he had a camera aimed my way. That infuriating smirk was still on his face.

What the hell?

I lifted my right hand and flipped him off. It wasn't like I'd ever be back here anyway.

"Perfect!" he called as he snapped my picture.

Chapter Two

"Why couldn't you be one of those models who doesn't eat? Then I wouldn't feel bad about having a job that pays peanuts."

"Great, now I'm hungry for peanuts," Kendra said. "Did you really give Flynn McCreary the finger?"

"I flipped the bird to a rude guy who interrupted the interview my beautiful, talented, understanding roommate set up for me," I countered.

We stood in our small apartment's kitchen with the empty cupboard doors hanging open around us. There was one box of pasta left and I was about to get creative with the remaining cans in our pantry.

It wasn't the first time we'd been in this situation and it wouldn't be the last.

Despite the lack of food, our apartment was my favorite place. The hardwood floors glowed in the sunshine and the old-fashioned wall sconce lighting added a soft glow in the evening. Kendra walked around turning the lamps on as I added water to our one pot. There was a built-in window seat that overlooked our busy street and a typical New York

City fire escape we had turned into a small, straggled garden.

Kendra watered two of the plants and then stretched out on the window seat. Her legs were so long she had to prop them up on the opposite wall and she smiled as she gazed outside.

We both loved it here.

Kendra had just been signed on to model for a swimwear line at Bouvier, but the money wouldn't come in for a while.

I wrote for a small creative firm, but I might as well write for peanuts for all the money I brought in. I kept hoping I'd luck out and land a serious job somehow, but for now, we were barely hanging on.

We'd been doing okay, but then our landlord had gotten sick.

He'd recovered, but it had hit home pretty hard, I guess. He was retiring to Florida and his son—the sleazoid from hell—was taking over.

"I'm telling you, we need to figure out who to call about this rent thing," I told Kendra. My gut was in a twist over what was happening. "I really don't think he can jack the rent up like that. And we both know he's doing it because he's pissed off you won't sleep with him."

The smile faded from Kendra's face and she turned her head. "What are you going to do? I keep calling the agency that's supposed to handle it and nobody is calling me back." Her shoulders sagged as she looked around the apartment. "We've only got two weeks before the money is due and if we don't pay, he'll throw us out. My grandma lived here since she was my age. I don't want to lose this place."

"I know." Feeling terrible that I'd ruined her good mood, I turned back to the food. "Look..." Then I shook my head. "Never mind."

Kendra would be fine once she started getting paid for her new modeling gig, but we needed money in the meantime. I'd still keep making phone calls to the agency though.

I stirred the water as she went back to the subject she wanted to discuss.

"I can't believe you flipped Flynn McCreary the bird."

Tossing her a grin, I shrugged. "I don't see why not. He was a jerk."

"That *jerk* is one of the most talented photographers at Bouvier."

"I know." I grinned at her. "It was all part of my grand scheme to become the world's next top hand model!"

"Oh, stop, Gabs." Kendra laughed and shook her head. "Was it really that bad?"

"On a scale of one to ten, it was a two thousand." I shuddered in mock terror as I reached for the pasta.

She beat me to it and put it back on the counter. "In that case, I owe you for your misery. How about a night out?"

"Did you miss the part where I didn't get the job?" I rolled my eyes. "I can't afford a night out."

"What about an exclusive party with free food

and drinks? Remember that swimwear gig I landed? They're having a launch party and I just happen to have two passes."

"Please tell me I don't have to wear a swimsuit," I said, switching off the stove immediately. For the chance to eat for free and not have to attempt to make do with what we had, I would've worn a tutu.

***

The blue dress Kendra loaned me wasn't hers.

I was above average height, but she had nearly six inches on me and while there were a few pieces of clothing we could swap out, anything that involved legs was pretty much a no-go. But the blue dress had been left over from a photo shoot and Kendra had a covetous love of clothes. If there was something left lying around and nobody took it, she did.

I'd come to love the habit, because it meant I could raid her closet and sometimes come out with pieces that would fit me. She wasn't quite as curvy as me—I was little over average in the bust and hip department—but she at least had something of a figure.

The blue dress came just a few inches short of my ass, and showed off more cleavage than it would have on a skinny model, but I didn't mind. The dance floor at the club was jammed and every time I looked around a new knot of men were orbiting us.

After the rejection of the interview and how Flynn had behaved, the attention felt good and I soaked it up like a sponge. I'd also had more than a few drinks, but after that lousy day, I told myself I was entitled.

A new song came on and a thickly muscled blond danced over to me.

"Hey, beautiful," he yelled over the music.

I shook my head at him and he took it as a sign to pull me close.

"You've got curves in all the right places. You two must be models, am I right?"

"She's the model," I said, still trying to be polite about it.

"Nuh, huh, baby, don't lie to me. I bet you're an underwear model. Much better than those skinny runway ones."

I gave him a bit of a push, but he didn't take the hint. He put about an inch between us, but kept dancing.

"Why do I have to be a model at all? Am I less attractive as a postal worker or a chef or a writer?" I asked, already knowing the answer.

"Models are hot," he said simply.

I know I should have taken it as the compliment he'd intended. Most women would be happy to be mistaken for an underwear model, or any kind of model. It wasn't easy hanging out with Kendra and keeping normal insecurities at bay. Maybe I didn't have my picture plastered on billboards, but I was a good looking woman. I was five-seven with good curves and I could eat what I liked—in moderation, of course—without worrying about hitting the treadmill the second I was done.

I pushed the blond guy away from me more forcefully this time and easily found another dance partner to bump against. This one just smiled down at my cleavage and didn't say anything.

Oh, well. Not like I expect to find Prince Charming here...

"You're a devil in that blue dress, honey."

A shiver raced up my spine and I turned. My brain kicked in a few seconds after my mouth, but what popped out hadn't exactly been thought through. "Nope...not the prince. It's the toad."

He cocked his head, familiar cadet blue eyes studying me. The free drinks I'd been imbibing had the room swirling under me and I started to regret them.

"The toad?" he asked, dark brown hair tumbling into his eyes. Stubble grazed his jaw. I tamped down the urge to rub my cheek against that sexy five o'clock shadow. Damn, he was hot.

"Yeah. The toad." I swallowed, suddenly feeling more tongue-tied than I liked. "You know. As in *Not Prince Charming.*"

He chuckled and moved closer. "Were you really looking for him here?"

We stood still in the writhing sea of dancers and just faced each other.

Before I could say anything else—reject Flynn's compliment, berate him for not giving me a chance at Bouvier—the blond guy returned and gave me a flirty hip check that knocked me off balance. Without looking like he'd even had to think about it, Flynn caught me around the waist and for one brief moment, my body was pressed to his as he steadied me. Breasts to chest, my belly to the flat concave of his, our thighs aligned down to the knee.

Oh, shit...

He held me there; that cocky smirk curving his lips.

A moment later, he was gone.

"Flynn McCreary, the toad." I muttered breathlessly. I told myself it was from the near-fall and not from the feel of Flynn's body so close to mine.

Kendra nodded in rhythm with the music before she twirled me around and waved at the bar. Flynn waved back and lifted a shot glass to me.

I scowled. "That's it. I'm going to find out why he axed me. I needed that job."

You weren't going to get it anyway, a small voice chided. I told the voice to shut up.

A new throng of suitors swept Kendra out of the way before she could stop me. I dodged dancers as I made my way across the crowded dance floor, disgusted as I saw Flynn smiling at my thwarted efforts. I narrowed my eyes at him and let a black-haired dancer with his shirt unbuttoned to his navel sweep me into a grinding turn. Flynn's smile slipped a little, but he gave me an appreciative nod as my oblivious dance partner presented my backside to him.

When I spun back around abruptly, it was to see his eyes still lingering where my ass had been.

Heat raced through me.

Breaking free of my dance partner, I marched up to Flynn and took the shot glass out of his hand, ignoring the surprised look on his face. I knocked back the stiff drink before bringing my still-wet lips to his ear.

"What's your problem with me?"

He turned slightly so that my mouth was at the corner of his. "You're not right for talent acquisition."

"You cost me that job!" I put as much venom in my voice as I could manage. It wasn't much. His aftershave flooded my head and I think it was potentially lethal. My knees were feeling weak already. Though that could've been the shot I'd just taken.

"Because I need you for a better one," he said.

Flynn took me by the waist and swung me onto his bar stool before ordering another round. I could still feel the heat from his hands and shifted, uncomfortable with my growing attraction. He took the opening and pushed to stand between my legs under the pretense of tipping the bartender. Despite the smell of him making me want to taste his neck, I put my hands on his shoulders and pushed him back, determined not to be distracted.

"What job?"

"Hand model," he said.

I almost snorted a laugh. "You're kidding. Did Kendra put you up to this?"

He shook his head and an irresistible strand of dark brown hair fell over his eyes. Before I could stop myself, I reached out and smoothed it back. He smiled down at me and I swiveled to grab the second whiskey shot he had ordered. He had to move back as I slammed back the shot and slid off the barstool.

He grabbed my hand before I could dive back into the crowd. As he raised it, for a moment, I thought he was going to kiss it, but he studied it instead, a serious expression on his face.

"You talk with your hands. I couldn't help but notice."

"Yeah, I'm not going to apologize about that," I said, unable to completely stop my smile at the memory of flipping him off.

He laughed and kissed the back of my hand, sending a jolt of electricity through me. Fuck. How did he do that?

"I wouldn't want you to. It's a great picture. Too bad the exec I showed it to won't let me use it in the new jewelry campaign." His eyes were sparkling.

"Why are you messing with me?" I asked, rolling my eyes. He was charming, all right, but still a dick.

"Stop by tomorrow. No joke."

Flynn gave me one more look and I felt every inch of it. He handed me an embossed card, clinked his whiskey shot against mine, drained it and then disappeared into the crowd.

I stared after him for a moment, not sure what

had just happened. Then Kendra was there, dragging me back onto the dance floor.

He was odd. Egocentric. Pushy. Arrogant.
And hot.
But odd.

***

"You have to go!" Kendra insisted. I'd just finished telling her about my insane encounter with Mr. Photographer.

"He really is a talented photographer and he offered you a job. Best case scenario, you get paid for a few hours of standing around holding your hands still."

"You know that's really hard for me," I started to argue despite the weakness of my point, then stopped. My eyes narrowed. "Wait, what's the worst case scenario?"

"That he hits on you and you like it." She gave me a devious grin and winked. "He's a notorious womanizer, Gabs. But hey, if you're curious... what's the harm?"

"Curious?" I stared at her. "Are you...saying I...?"

She grinned for a moment and then went back to the ritual of her weekly manicure, ignoring the fact that I was still gaping at her.

Curious...that made me think about things I didn't need to think about.

That made me think about Flynn.

Made me think about *me* and *Flynn*.

The two of us. Together. Naked. Those long-fingered, elegant hands of his running over me. My mouth went dry just picturing it.

"No." I lied through my teeth. "I'm not curious. Not about Flynn McCreary."

***

Kendra's words echoed in my head Monday morning as I walked into the address printed on Flynn's business card. The warehouse space was divided into a chic boutique of pale fashionable clothes and an art gallery featuring sketches of designer handbags.

The bored receptionist pointed up the stairs when I told her who I was here to see. The photography studio stretched out the entire second floor with windows the entire length of the street view.

"Mr. McCreary?"

"I detect a little accent, Tennessee. Does that mean you're nervous?"

I gave him the finger and he laughed. "I've already got that pose. Come on. I've got other things in mind."

Fighting the urge to fidget, I lowered my hand and stood there, feeling lost in the vast space. He crossed over to me and cupped the offending hand in both of his, using it to draw me towards the far

21

corner where the windows were covered, creating a darkened—or darker—area.

There, a white pedestal waited in front of what looked like a giant white screen. A backdrop, I remembered. Dozens of lights aimed at the spot from what I guessed were strategic places.

"Please, let me make you more comfortable."

"I'd be more comfortable knowing what the hell I'm doing here," I said bluntly.

Without answering my question, he gently pulled both my hands onto the pedestal and began massaging them. The deep rub of his thumbs in the center of my palms released a pressure I hadn't realized was trapped there. The heat of the friction and the slow, deliberate circles soon uncoiled something else. Heat flared in my stomach, quickly traveling south until it pooled between my legs.

I swallowed. Tensing, I tried to pull away as heat rushed to my face.

He didn't release my hands, keeping a light hold on them. "No, no. You can relax. You have to be relaxed for this job."

"What job?" I asked, as much to keep my attention from how good his hands felt around mine as anything else.

He answered without looking at me even as he released my hands. "A new jewelry line called Delicate. I can't have you cupping an eggshell if you're so tense."

He went over to the long table and picked up an egg, two egg shells, and a diamond tennis bracelet.

Flynn then walked up behind me and reached around either side of me. He clasped the dazzling bracelet around my left wrist and carefully placed two broken halves of an eggshell in my fingertips. It seemed a bit strange, but he was the artist.

"Alright, put your other hand flat here. It'll help you stay steady and it'll add to the background. Your skin is perfect, almost translucent."

I tried to ignore the tickle of his breath on my neck as he leaned in closer and posed my right hand. He then smoothed the large diamonds along my wrist and the slight caress sent shivers up my arm. I steeled myself not to move and prayed goosebumps wouldn't give me away.

Don't screw this job up too, Gabs. Just because you haven't gotten any in a while...

He stepped back and picked up his camera. A few rapid-fire shots and he put it down. This time he ran his fingers down my arm in order to gently rearrange the angle of my wrist. His dark brown hair brushed my cheek and I decided to look out the window and pretend I was writing a scene, something that had nothing to do with attractive men and how good they smelled.

"You've got a soft touch, Ms. Baine. I think I may be jealous of an eggshell."

"The bracelet is part of my payment, right?" I asked. I'd just blurted it out, not really expecting an answer. I was finding it increasingly difficult to think around him.

He chuckled and added finely shredded pale

blue tissue paper to one of the empty eggshell halves. He leaned over to delicately place a pair of diamond earrings on top of the paper and his fashionably unbuttoned shirt fell open. I couldn't help seeing his chiseled chest and that made me wonder what a fashion photographer did to work out. My mind betrayed me and immediately imagined him doing push-ups over me. Dammit. I really needed to get laid.

"Relax a little. You're doing beautifully, Gabriella."

I liked the way my name sounded in that deep voice of his.

A few more rapid-fire shots and he removed all the props from my hands.

"Tedious work but, trust me, I'll make your hands look good."

"Good, otherwise I won't be able to show my face around town," I quipped as I began to stretch my fingers. My breath caught when Flynn took my hand between his and began to help. I kept talking to prevent me from thinking about the way his fingers were manipulating mine. "Does this mean I can't do high-fives anymore? I mean, now that you're going to make me a famous hand model?"

Flynn caught my eyes, his warm hands still caressing mine. "How about I get us something to drink?"

I shrugged, trying to be noncommittal, and he smiled at me as he walked away. I ignored the stab of disappointment and began to pace around, desperate to cool down the molten feeling in my muscles before he came back. He moved with a lean, powerful grace that had me itching to touch him.

He's a notorious womanizer...

Kendra's voice echoed in my ear and I had to swallow back a groan.

All I could think about was his hard body leaning into mine at the club the other night. Today, his dark brown hair was slicked back and his face was smooth. He smelled faintly of that amazing aftershave and it made the urge to rub my cheek along his jaw line even harder to resist.

I shook my head and distracted myself with a long white table of portfolio folders. Reaching for the nearest one, I flipped it open.

"Oh, you might not want to do that," Flynn said from behind me.

"Do what?" I asked as I flipped open the first portfolio.

He smirked as he gestured to the table. "That."

Confused, I looked down. As my brain registered what my eyes were seeing, my mouth fell open.

Chapter Three

My cheeks turned red once I realized his warning had been more of a tease than anything else.

The portfolio was filled with black and white photographs of nude models. I flipped through a few, trying to cool my embarrassment. I wasn't some prude or naïve little girl to be freaked out over a couple of nude photographs, although...wow. This wasn't some nude portrait hanging in an art gallery. These were *hot*.

Flynn edged closer, so close I could feel his body heat.

"You like what you see?" Flynn's tone was half-mocking, half-seducing. "Want to take a few in the dark room for further study?"

"Don't be a child," I snapped.

"Oooh, there's that Southern drawl," he said.

He was teasing me, but I couldn't take my eyes off the photographs. They were not gratuitous, models posed for exploitation or just to please the lustful eye. They were beautiful studies of the female form, beautiful and sensual. One photograph conveyed such a sense of vulnerability I ached for her. Another such ferociousness that I wished it could be imprinted in my mind to banish any lingering insecurities. The angle said as much about the photographer as the nude pose revealed about the model. Despite myself, I was fascinated.

"Here, let me help." He dabbed my chin with a paper napkin. "You got a little drool there."

I slapped his hand away, but without any real malice. My cheeks were burning, but not from the pictures anymore. "You must be the photographer's twelve year-old son."

"Ouch." Flynn smiled as he put his hand over his heart.

I collected myself, determined to show him that I could be more mature about this than he was. "So you take nude photos on the side. Just for fun or are you getting ready for a gallery show?"

He snorted in derision as he tugged the portfolio from me and flipped it open, bending over to study it closely. I could only see his face in profile, but it was clear that he was looking at his work with a far more critical eye than I thought they deserved. Even the more erotic ones that left me blushing were incredibly lovely.

"Why do you take them?" I asked again.

He looked over at me, a grin tugging up the corner of his lips. "Why the hell not?"

He flipped the portfolio closed and shrugged before cutting to go around me.

There was an abruptness to his movements that made me realize that somehow, I'd put a wall between us. Or he had. I wasn't sure how I felt about that.

"How do you find models to pose nude?" I asked suddenly. Then I grimaced, realizing how naïve that sounded.

He gave a short mirthless laugh, but his expression changed when he realized I was serious. He jerked a shoulder in a shrug. "It pays better."

I knew I'd hate myself for asking, but now I was curious. "How much is better?"

"How much is on the books for your hand modeling gig today, three hundred?" He cocked up a brow as he waited for me to nod. Then he angled his head toward the portfolio full of nudes. "Model for a nude? It can bring in three thousand or more."

Shit. "That's..." I cleared my throat. "That's a lot of money."

I turned to look out the windows so he couldn't read on my face what was going on in my head. With Kendra not getting paid for a couple weeks and my current job not paying me much of anything, it was hard not to think about it. I told myself that I was already doing the hand model gig because I needed the cash, but the idea of ten times that amount kept running through my head.

Apparently, he didn't need to see my face to know what I was thinking.

"Tempting, huh?" The sly arrogance came back into his voice. "Or maybe now that you have the taste for modeling, you can't get enough?"

He came around, putting himself between me and the window, grinning at me. The attitude was confusing. Insulting. How could the sensitivity I'd seen in those images come from somebody so deliberately crass, someone almost cruel?

It had to be an act, but I couldn't see why. He was talented and didn't need to act like an ass. The biggest problem, however, was his words sounded like a challenge and I had never been able to turn down a dare. I wanted to strip off all my clothes and make him blush.

"What are you thinking?" he asked, his voice a low murmur.

"Go away." I turned back to stare out the window. He chuckled and I could hear him moving around behind me.

"You didn't answer. You know, it can be a bit of a rush—"

Spinning on my heel, I glared at him.

Flash—

Lights went off. He snapped another one as I folded my arms over my chest and leveled a glare on him.

He let out a low whistle. "Damn. You could burn someone with those nutmeg brown eyes, babe." He straightened and gave me a once over. "I'll pay you the three thousand if you show me what you've got."

Three thousand...

For a second, all I could do was stare at him.

Then, as the shock faded and the urge to tell him

to kiss my ass faded, reason kicked in. Three thousand. That would keep us level until Kendra started seeing payments from her modeling contract. It would tide us over between my meager checks.

I thought of the beautiful images I'd seen in the portfolio and swallowed. My face heated and my heart started to pound.

It wasn't like he was asking me to sleep with him.

They are just pictures.

"Well?" His mouth curled up in a smile. Then he shrugged. "Didn't think so."

Jerk.

I curled my lip at him and leaned against the nearby table, steadying myself as I took off my boot. If he thought I was too shy and backward to do this, then I'd show him a thing or two.

Once I had my boot in hand, I threw it at him.

He dodged the boot, flashed me a blue-eyed dare and took more pictures. I could tell by the look on his face that he was enjoying himself. I didn't know if I wanted him to or not. I tossed the other boot over my shoulder, refusing to cringe as I heard it clatter across the table. I never claimed to have good aim.

He smirked from behind the lens. "That all you got, Tennessee?"

"Maybe that's all you deserve," I retorted. "Maybe I should have put one of those boots where the sun don't shine." I let my drawl come out on the last bit.

"What about all these buttons?" he asked. "Bet you could be cruel with those."

I stilled as he came towards me, unsure of what to expect. My entire body tensed as he fingered each of the small pearl buttons on my blouse before pushing back my hair and then standing back to snap another picture. I felt my face burning and couldn't deny that a not-so-small part of it was arousal.

He didn't think I could pull it off. How many women could do a slow strip tease in broad daylight, much less a sunlight-filled studio? I was willing to bet his skinny models simpered and giggled, more worried about flirting with him than anything else. Hell with that.

I walked towards him, seeing the scene unfold as though I were writing it. As I moved, I undid two buttons at the bottom of my shirt. He crouched down, angling the lens up and I stopped, slowly and deliberately popping the button on my jeans, exposing the pale skin of my stomach.

"So good," he muttered. "I love close-ups."

He reached out and photographed his own hand sliding up my inner thigh. It suddenly became hard to breathe as his touch burned through my jeans. He set the camera aside and, without coming out of his crouch, gripped my waistband and gave it a bit of a tug.

"Any chance you'll take these off?"

I realized the up-close of me trying to wriggle

free of my skinny jeans wasn't going to do anything for his pictures or my ego so I backed away and regrouped.

I wasn't rail thin like a traditional model. I had curves, hips, boobs...I could play to my strengths, but those strengths didn't involve wiggling and shimmying out of my jeans right in front of that camera.

I turned back and pulled open the top buttons of my shirt. With the middle two buttons still holding, I slipped one arm out of my shirt and then the other, clutching the remaining fabric to my almost fully exposed chest. The clutching only amplified my cleavage and I watched as his gaze zoomed in, right on target.

"Yes, great." Flynn took a half dozen rapid-fire shots, then lowered the camera, silent for a moment as if he was trying to figure something out. "Lay down," he finally said. When I didn't immediately move, he added, "Trust me."

My heart was racing, but I knew it would be foolish to stop at this point. After all, he was a professional photographer and I had seen his work. None of those women had looked coerced or bothered by what they were doing. And, if I was going to be completely honest with myself, I knew if I backed down now, he'd have won. I was competitive enough to hate that idea.

I lifted my chin and walked over to the pile of cushions and blankets he'd motioned to. They were the same ones that the other models had been on, but as I stretched out, I began to feel self-conscious.

That feeling only grew as he joined me and without a word, stood on the cushions, one foot on either side of my knees. Picture after picture, he changed the angle of the camera, bending down low, then straightening.

After a couple minutes, he put the camera down and dropped to his knees over me. His face was flushed. His eyes burned. He probably just got really into his work.

I tried to pretend it was because of me, though.

Why should I be the only one affected?

I caught my breath as he reached down and unzipped my jeans, then took hold of the waistband. His gaze lingered on my face a moment, giving me the chance to protest.

When I didn't, he drew the jeans down, leaving me in a pair of simple lace panties.

Why hadn't I put on something sexier?

I looked up to find his eyes lingering on the dip of my waist, the flare of my hip, roaming over me with a heat that left me feeling lightheaded. As he sat back on his heels, I levered myself up and let my shirt fall completely away.

Sitting there in a bra that matched my panties, I stared at him. My pulse raced so hard, it was a wonder he didn't hear it.

He snapped a picture, then reached up and pushed my hair back over my shoulders, snapped several more, pausing here and there to adjust the angle of my chin or to mutter a command. "Look toward the wall...now at me. Smile...no, not like that. Think about the first time you were kissed...that bad, huh? Okay, think about *me* kissing you...perfect..."

He lowered the camera while I was still breathing heavy from the thought of kissing him and he came closer, reached up and hooked his finger under my bra strap. After a moment, he slowly pulled it down.

My nipples were already tight, but at the feel of his skin against mine, I gasped. With the strap of my bra hanging down my shoulder, he eased back and lifted the camera.

"Take the bra off now. Slowly..."

Goosebumps broke out across my skin as I did it.

I wasn't even thinking now.

Thought had left the building so long ago, it was insane.

I slid the straps over my shoulders, keeping one arm over my breasts as I tossed the bra off to the side.

"Good...perfect...look down...now, up at me."

I did.

He lifted his eyes from behind his camera and stared.

Waited.

Without him saying a word, I knew what he wanted. He began snapping pictures as I slowly lowered my arm, revealing myself to him and his camera. I thought I saw his fingers tighten on the camera, but he didn't say anything. My nipples drew tighter still, throbbing and aching and I couldn't understand it, but I was more turned on than I'd ever been in my life.

"Will you lay back?" he asked.

There wasn't even a hint of professionalism in his tone now—his voice was ragged, rough and for some reason, that made it easier to lie back, bracing my weight on my elbows.

"Bring up your knee."

I did and when he next had me roll onto my side, I did that as well, following him with my eyes as he came around to crouch next to the bed. "Pull your hair forward. Have it curling around your nipples. I want the contrast of auburn against your skin."

My breath came out in a low, shaky sound as I did just that and I had to bite my inner cheek to keep from gasping as I smoothed my hair down.

"No. Here..."

He came closer.

I froze as he reached out.

His eyes held mine for the longest moment and then he started to stroke, smoothing my hair so my left nipple played peekaboo. He remained there a minute, adjusting the sheets, then me, his fingers lingering on my skin.

He snapped two or three shots and then lowered the camera. "Panties."

Slowly, I rolled to my back and slid them off, trying not to think of the ways I was exposing myself. I tossed them aside and put my legs back

36

down.

The camera stopped and lowered. He chewed the inside of his cheek for a moment, his eyes roving over my body. Heat burned there, the kind of heat that somehow managed to banish any insecurities I should have had.

A thrill began to surge inside me and I wanted to stretch out before him, exhilarate in the headiness this was giving me. He moved closer. Firm hands took mine, guiding me. I stayed calm, or at least appeared calm as he posed me, arranging me how he wanted.

I twisted this way and that at his command as the camera fired away. I lost all sense of time and any inhibitions I'd had melted away under his careful instruction.

The sunlight moved across the warm studio and I lost all track of time. He took a few last photographs and took a step back as he set down his camera.

His eyes were sparkling as he spoke, "Now how about some fun?"

Chapter Four

He left me standing in the middle of the studio naked.

Okay...that's not exactly what I'd seen coming.

I'd assumed *fun* would entail sex. After all, he was supposed to be this big time flirt. A lady killer, right?

I was so worked up, if he'd decided to seduce me, I wouldn't have minded. Actually, I was on board with the idea. I was no virgin and I wasn't afraid of my own sexuality. After all, I had taken his dare and had actually enjoyed it.

Should I feel embarrassed now? Exploited or something?

I'd just posed naked for money.

Abruptly, I realized I *did* feel a little embarrassed, and out of place. Grabbing one of the blankets on the bed, I wrapped it around myself and started to pace. Drifting up and down the studio, I let my eyes wander to the framed prints on the wall. They were advertisements, some of them for small local places, but others were for national brands that I'd heard of even back in Tennessee.

It made me feel better. Flynn wasn't doing any of this to sell to some cheap skin magazine.

Bouvier was top-of-the-line fashion and the name itself was synonymous with elegance. If my naked body ended up in one of their advertisements, it would be tasteful.

Maybe I could get some shots worth putting into a portfolio. Kendra had been telling me I could be a catalog model. I'd always assumed that she was just being polite. Typically, women who looked like me ended up getting hired as plus-sized models. In this society, anything over a size eight was considered plus-sized, but that's the fashion world for you. I refused to perpetuate that way of thinking.

I'd never thought much about it when she told me I should consider trying to find any agent, but maybe she was serious. I definitely wasn't cut out for *her* world, but there were other options.

Maybe modeling was a possibility. Apparently Flynn saw something in me.

As I was considering the drastic career change, Flynn returned with a crate and pulled out half a dozen small jars.

I gave him a curious look and he grinned.

"Body paint!"

The devilish look was back in his cadet blue eyes though now I could see he forced it. Something had happened during our intimate photo shoot and he wanted to put it out of his mind. He wanted to put me back in one of the regular places woman usually held in his life: easy fun or pure art.

I shook my head. "Nice try, sleazeball, but you're not turning me into cheap performance art."

He grinned. The blanket I'd wrapped around my torso and tucked in near my breasts chose that moment to loosen and gape, drooping down to my waist.

I caught it, but before I could cover back up, Flynn came over and tugged it away.

I wasn't about to get into a wrestling match after all the work I'd done to convince him of my nonchalant attitude so I gave it up with a bored sigh. "I'm not letting you put a bunch of paint all over me," I said again.

"Oh, come on, it won't hurt a bit." He lifted a brow as he added, "You want the three thousand, right?"

I swallowed down the urge to growl at him. "What exactly did you have in mind?"

He smiled.

A few moments later, I wish I had stuck by my *no*.

I held still as he lifted gloved hands, covered in brilliant red, toward my torso. "Don't move," he said. His eyes lingered on my face. "You don't want it to run."

I swallowed and held still.

He'd had me pull my hair up and now I stood in front of him, naked, without even the illusion of modesty my long hair could provide. When he cupped my breasts in his paint-slicked hands, I gasped.

"There's one."

I didn't breathe as he backed away and changed the gloves, pressing them into a vivid purple this time.

He pressed one palm to my neck. The other to my abdomen. But instead of stripping off the gloves, he dipped them back into the small pool of paint he'd poured out and, a moment later, I had a purple palm print on my right ass cheek and another one on my left hip.

The pattern continued. A blue palm above my pubis, along my right thigh. Orange on my right hip and left knee.

It didn't take that long, but I was practically panting for a release that wouldn't come when he backed away and started to take pictures. He stopped after only a couple and came back, releasing my hair from the ponytail. He stood so close his chest touched my nipples.

A weak whimper left my lips.

His eyes came to mine.

My heart stopped for a moment and we were both still.

The hand that had been smoothing my hair down tightened in it. "Gabriella," he muttered, just before he caught my mouth in a searing kiss. I couldn't stop the moan as his tongue turned delicious circles around my own.

Without breaking the kiss, he pulled off his shirt and I wondered if he purposefully wore ones that buttoned so he could take off his clothes while still managing a knee-weakening kiss. Flinging his shirt aside, he raised his head. We were both breathing heavily and his eyes darkened as he glanced down at my breasts, marked by the mostly-dried red paint he'd placed on me.

His mouth came back to mine, but he didn't linger. Instead, he began to move in a line down my chin, my neck, along the midline of my chest.

When he went to his knees in front of me, I started to tremble. One hand gripped my left hip, almost exactly where he'd placed the palm print earlier. The other curved around my waist, again mirroring a painted palm print.

"I've been dying to touch you like this," he said, his voice guttural. "I've wanted it from the first time I saw you."

The fading light outside made our faint reflection appear in the nearby windows and I watched us, watched as his hands made my body burn. I knew I should put a stop to it. I was letting myself become a cliché, seduced by a known womanizer.

"They're mirrored," he said, misreading the expression on my face. "We can see out, but no one can see in."

He stood back up, bringing my mouth to his with a forceful tug on my hair. As his tongue tangled around mine, my brain kept telling me to stop, to hold onto my self-respect.

His cock was hard, throbbing against me, but it didn't matter if he wanted me and it didn't matter how good it felt to have his hands stroking my back, my hips, my ass.

Stop, I told myself. *You need to stop...*

But even as I finally pulled up the strength to do it, he looked down at me, a puzzled look on his face. It was as though he didn't know what was going on, as if he'd never touched a woman, kissed a woman. As if he didn't know what to make of me.

And when he came back to kiss me again, I couldn't bear to pull away.

When he lowered me onto the hardwood floor, I didn't resist. I lay there, looking up at him as he finished what I'd attempted to start before. He stripped out of his pants with smooth expedience and in moments, he was coming down on top of me, naked and hard.

It was my turn to look, I thought as I greedily devoured the sight of him. Damn, he was beautiful. The v-grooves of his hips and the thin trail of dark curls that started at his bellybutton all pointed towards a thick, swollen shaft. It was perfectly shaped, curving up towards his belly. Long, but not too long. The right size to make me feel every inch, but not so big that he'd have to be careful. And thick...sinfully thick. The sight of him made me swallow and I squirmed a little, thinking of having him inside me.

He caught my knees and slowly pushed my thighs apart, his eyes on my face the entire time. My breath hitched as he cupped me, bold and blatant, using his middle finger to stroke the pulsing point of my clitoris.

I shivered. He smiled at my response. He came down over me and started to massage my clit even as he began to circle my entrance with another finger.

"You're already wet," he whispered. He watched me as he pushed inside and I sucked in a breath, pressing my palms flat to the floor.

He hissed in a breath as he began to stroke me with his finger, soft and shallow at first, then faster and deeper.

Arousal sparked sharply when he added a second finger and curled them, withdrawing completely so that I felt every single inch.

I started to rock up to meet his hand, panting, whimpering...and he stopped.

I heard the unmistakable sound of a condom wrapper ripping and opened my eyes, locking with his. Without looking away, he pushed his hands underneath my buttocks and opened me further. The tip of his erection teased me, slid back and forth along my clitoris and then, slowly, he pushed inside.

I stared into his eyes and tried not to beg. I needed more.

With one smooth stroke, he moved forward, filling me even as I cried out. He held himself still inside my body and I could feel him throbbing as he waited, either for his own control or my adjustment.

His mouth found mine again as he rocked slowly against me. I clutched his shoulders as I slid my tongue between his lips. He began to thrust, long, deep strokes that made me whimper and moan.

He took each sound into his mouth, swallowing them down.

His teeth caught my bottom lip, worrying at it until I dug my nails into his shoulders. He kissed his way down my throat and the air was filled with the sounds of pleasure I couldn't control.

My climax came with a suddenness that took my breath away, my legs shaking, my entire body convulsing in one coil and release of ecstasy. It hit hard and fast, stealing my breath away and Flynn slowed, his movements easing for a moment.

I sucked in oxygen, my head spinning.

Once I was no longer seeing stars, he caught my thigh in his hand, lifting my leg as he started to surge against me, hard and fast. I cried up in surprise. He buried his face against my neck, his cock an iron brand throbbing inside me.

He muttered something that sounded like my name and then drove himself into me faster and harder than before. The wild rhythm brought me to another peak and we came together in a tight tangle of limbs and sweat and fire.

He slid down and dropped his head to rest between my breasts.

I tried to steady my breathing, dazed delight spinning through my head.

Whoa...

That was the only thought in my head.

Whoa...

I'd had sex before and I'd enjoyed it before. Or so I'd thought. But this...*whoa*...this had been *pure lust.*

I didn't dare to wonder how I stacked up against what must have been a considerable list of his previous partners, but I could say that the few other lovers in my past had been fumbling, awkward teenagers compared to him. I was about to say something when he pulled away and sat up, his face set in grim lines.

He flicked a glance at me and I caught sight of the anger there. My blood froze. I had the oddest feeling the anger was directed at himself, not me, but still, the sight of it made my belly churn.

He pushed himself to his feet, not looking at me. "I'll call down to the front desk and they'll have the cash for you."

He turned his back on me as he walked to a stack of towels sitting on a nearby table and tossed one my way.

"Shower's in there," he said coolly, jerking his head over his shoulder. "Make it fast."

"I..."

He lifted his head, staring at me with ice in his gaze.

I grabbed my clothes and ducked into the room I hadn't noticed until now. Shaking, I pressed my back to the wall and looked around. The bathroom was elegant and upscale and the toiletries would have probably blown my mind if I had been capable of thought. Instead, though, I was in a state of numbness as I washed up, the paint washing off easily under the spray of water.

When I came out, Flynn had already dragged on a pair of jeans and was on the phone.

He caught sight of me and turned his back.

Fury lit inside me—finally.

That *ass*.

As I continued to stand there, he looked back at me and I heard his sigh, listening to him say, "Hold on."

"I told you, money's down at the desk."

"I ought to just tell you to shove that money up your ass," I snapped. I had my pride.

Jerking up my chin, I strode past him. I should do it.

He was already talking to whoever when I slammed the door shut behind me.

The rent was due—*soon*.

I was flat broke. And Flynn probably wouldn't notice anyway, which would make the whole statement a moot point.

I walked down the steps at war with myself.

I hesitated at the bottom of the steps and just as I started to head toward the door, a woman looked up, a smile on her face. "Ms. Baine?"

I froze.

She came out from behind the desk, an envelope in hand. "Your fee."

Slowly, I took it.

Rent. Electricity. Groceries, I told myself. He'd offered me the money before we'd had sex. I was being paid for modeling. Not for what had happened after. They were two different things.

I pasted a fake smile on my face and left as quickly as I could. I didn't plan on *ever* going back there.

Chapter Five

My memory of the Flynn incident swung back and forth like a heavy pendulum of guilt and pride.

On one side, I was devastated that I had let myself be drawn in by such a cheap ploy. I thought I was smarter than that.

But on the other I could still feel the aftershocks from my climax.

Was I really just a naïve girl who let a manipulating bastard take advantage of her?

I was a free, adult woman who took her pleasure when the opportunity arose.

It was enough to give me a headache.

The one thing I couldn't do was let myself think about the look I'd seen in Flynn's eyes—that one brief flicker of something I'd thought was real. I didn't know if there had been any real emotion there or not, but whatever it had been, he'd buried it deep and I wasn't going to try to dig it out, no matter how good the sex had been.

The worst part was that I lied to Kendra that evening when I handed her the money.

"You sold a treatment for a new show? That is so

great! I'm so proud of you." She threw her arms around me.

"It's not really a big deal. I managed to do my job," I said, grateful she couldn't see my face.

"It's going to be a hit, I know it. What's it about?" She released me, still beaming from ear to ear.

"A romantic comedy?" It came out like a question.

"You're not sure?" Kendra asked, confused.

I sighed. "Because it's not the truth. I lied."

I collapsed against our kitchen counter. Kendra leaned against the opposite side and crossed her arms, the expression on her face saying she was waiting for an explanation.

I still couldn't tell her the truth. "It was just the script for a commercial. Not even a good commercial. One of those awful acne cream ads where all the people talk about ugly ducklings and other fairytale bullshit."

"Oh, who cares, Gabs." She rolled her eyes. "You're doing what you love and you're making it work. We can pay rent!"

"And buy groceries," I added.

More than the lie, I felt what Kendra said get under my skin.

She was proud of me for doing what I loved. Except I hadn't done any of it.

"Yay to groceries," I said, forcing myself to smile. "I'm going to splurge...I'm getting ice cream."

***

I didn't sleep worth crap. It wasn't until the cool, quiet hours of early morning that I understood why I was so uneasy.

Kendra had been so excited for me because she thought I was making money doing something I loved.

Instead, I'd taken off my clothes, had some pictures taken, then had sex with a man who'd set my body on fire. That wasn't what had me crashing though.

It was the look on his face after.

I should have stayed.

I should have pushed him, fought with him. Something.

Instead, I'd let the hurt inside me win.

I'd given up. Even though I felt something between us, I'd given up.

I thought about the look I'd seen in his eyes. The entire reason I'd let him pull me down to the floor when the voice of reason had told me to pull away. That intense, strange expression on his face as though he had no idea who I was or what he was doing there. It was as though he had been seeing *me* for the first time.

But when he'd freaked out, what had I done?

"I ran," I muttered.

Here I was, still stuck in my dead-end job, not doing much of anything that I'd dreamed about.

Then I end up having the kind of sex girls only can dream of and when it went to shit, did I do anything to find out why? No. *I fucking ran.*

It was like I was just giving up on everything I'd always expected to find in my life.

I was wallowing on the couch when Kendra burst through the door with a bag of colorful ribbons and tissue paper. My eyebrows shot up. It was a rare day when she was up before me, and an even rarer one when her chestnut brown curls weren't perfectly styled, but rather pulled back into a sloppy ponytail.

"My cousin's son turns two next week. Look! I got him finger paint."

I stared at the bright colors. The red, the blue, the orange...

"I lied!"

For a moment, Kendra just looked at me. Then she put the gift and trimmings down and went into the kitchen. I stayed where I was. After all, in the studio apartment we shared, the kitchen was just on the other side of the big, open room. Hugging my knees to my chest, I watched her.

Dramatic confessions were nothing new here.

We both had a penchant for drama. It was just my turn this time.

"So. Details," she said calmly.

"I did the whole hand modeling gig. That much was real," I said. "And I knew he probably flirted with everyone. It just felt good."

"It's okay to flirt and it's even okay to have sex. You're both consenting adults. Don't be so hard on yourself, Gabriella." Kendra smiled at me as she pulled two cups down out of the cabinet.

"Yeah, but I let him pay me to take naked photographs!" My face flamed at the admission.

She didn't even blink. "For Bouvier. If anything, you could make a career out of it. I told you, you're beautiful. It's possible you could hit it in modeling and if anybody can make it happen, it's Flynn McCreary."

"He didn't believe I would do it," I said sheepishly. "You know how I like a dare. And then he brought out body paint and, I don't know, it just escalated from there."

"And there's nothing wrong with that," Kendra said and then shook her head. "You're not going to forgive yourself, are you?"

"For doing exactly what I judged other women for doing? Nope."

"I'm so sorry, Gabs. I keep putting you in these awful situations," Kendra said, pouring two cups of hot water and adding in tea bags.

I continued with my confession. "And then when I lied, you were so proud of me for my writing and I realized I was ignoring what I really want out of life. I mean...there's the writing, which is going to shit. And there's my love life...which doesn't exist."

Sighing, I braced my elbow on the back of the couch and stared outside. "I don't want sexy little flings, no matter how blue the man's eyes are. I want love, the whole romance and flowers and everything kind of love. Ugh. I'm so naïve!"

"It's not naïve." Kendra came down and sat beside me. Shoulder-bumping me, she said, "Love's kind of the thing. We all want it. I'd even be willing to bet asshats like Flynn want love. They just don't know how to get it. And that's the difference. You do and you can."

"Yeah?" I glowered into my tea cup. "Then where's my Prince Charming?"

"Still waiting for you to find him, Cinderella." She grinned at me. "Come on. You need to cheer up. There's this party—"

I stopped her. "This sounds familiar. A lot like the last time where I came out with a hand modeling job at the studio of sin."

"Yeah, it is an industry party." She laughed. "They're celebrating all the up-and-comers."

"You mean you?" I asked.

"Well, yes." She glowed. "Apparently, I'm finally an up-and-comer. Open bar, free food."

"More like all I can eat because other models only peck at it."

She grinned. "That's my Gabs! Come on, it'll be fun."

My stomach twisted as something occurred to me. "What if he's there?"

"No chance," Kendra said. "Word has it he's off to Europe. I heard the project director for the swimwear line complaining about how much he can get away with just because he's Flynn McCreary."

"Then count me in," I said.

***

I was glad I'd agreed.

I'd never been to this sort of party before.

It was the kind people could see from miles away, thanks to laser light shows and the spotlights bursting from neighboring buildings.

Then there was a red carpet. An actual red carpet. Kendra's agent had sent over a gigantic SUV with silver spinning rims and when it pulled up to the velvet ropes, Kendra grabbed my hand and pulled me out. I had no choice but to follow her down that red carpet, trying not to look too dazzled...and trying not to fall or stumble too much in the extra-high heels she'd loaned me.

Inside, still blinking from all the flashbulbs, I was left alone as Kendra was swept away by a flock of reed-thin models. I managed to snag a glass of champagne from a passing waiter and tell myself that I loved to play the part of the mysterious outsider. I was just working up a back-story for my fashion correspondent turned film producer when I was interrupted.

"I saw you on the red carpet with Kendra Facet, didn't I?"

I started to turn with a snarky comment since I was sure I was about to be asked to be a go-between. Ice blue eyes looked down on me from a handsome, chiseled face and I swallowed the snark.

"Yes, she's my roommate. She invited me. I'm

not just making that up." I had the feeling I was starting to babble.

He laughed, the sound warm and inviting. He was tall, easily six-three, six-four, and dressed in a conservative, yet expensive suit. As good-looking as he was, he didn't look like a model or have the searching look of an agent finding an angle. That meant he was probably one of the countless executives that kept the fashion industry in the billions of dollars.

"My name's Edward." He held out his hand.

"Nice to meet you. I'm Gabriella." I took it, smiling at the little tingle of warmth that went through me.

"Kendra's roommate."

"That's me," I said.

He smiled again and sipped his drink though I could see his eyes traveling down the outfit Kendra had carefully chosen. It was one of the few things of hers that could actually fit me, though I filled it out quite a bit more than she did.

I waited, assuming he was trying to find a way to bring up Kendra again. I would've done it myself just to get it over with, but here he was, speaking to me and I wasn't certain I wanted to end that just yet—then I'd go back to playing the mysterious outsider.

"You come here often?" I asked.

He laughed, that deep sensual sound, and I felt it tangle in my stomach. Wow. That was some laugh.

"Yes, actually. It's kind of a family obligation."

He looked down at me and I saw something in those blue eyes shift, as if making some sort of internal decision. "Would you like to dance, Gabriella?"

We passed our glasses off onto a passing server and moved onto the dance floor. Each step, each moment erased the Flynn incident a little more. Edward made comments about people I pointed out, never anything rude but always interesting. As people came up and tried to interrupt us, he introduced me and then waved them away, keeping his arms loosely around me the entire time.

He was something straight out of a fairytale. It was like I'd kissed the toad and here I was with Prince Charming. It was easier to believe in things like love...or at least romance again.

After a couple songs, he leaned over my hand and kissed the back of it. The feel of his lips on the back of my hand had warmth racing through me and I fought a dopey sigh.

"I apologize, Gabriella, but if I don't mingle, people will start to talk."

He winked at me and waited for me to let him go. I did so with a smile then watched as model after model deliberately threw herself in his path. When he walked up to Kendra, my smile faded and I told myself that was it. He had finally found the one he'd been looking for, and I'd be forgotten, just another dance. Then Kendra's eyes caught mine and she smiled. They leaned towards each other and looked at me as they spoke. My stomach flipped. They were talking about me.

As the night waned on, I heard his name brought up over and over.

"He was just featured on the Forbes list again," an agent said—I knew her vaguely. She'd tried to approach Kendra and when she saw me, she turned her back.

"Too bad he's never listed as a most-eligible bachelor," her friend added.

I covertly studied him and because I was doing so, it wasn't hard to notice that I wasn't the only one. A couple of Kendra's friends, somebody I suspected was another agent, a few more models.

I tried not to listen to the idle gossip and add to it my own ideas. I heard nothing *but* gossip and when I finally caught up with Kendra, she didn't know who he was, either. Then again, she was drunk enough I was surprised she remembered who I was.

The one thing I *did* know was that everywhere I went, his eyes always seemed to find me. Once or twice we'd raised our glasses and smiled, but he kept his distance.

At the end of the night, or more accurately, early morning, I was following Kendra into the town car when she mentioned him.

"He likes you."

"What?" I half fell attempting to get her into the car without falling. Once she collapsed inside, I paused outside the door to take off my—*her*—shoes.

"The gorgeous tall guy. The one you danced with. He couldn't take his eyes off you."

"Did too many glasses of wine turn you into a

60

ten year old? Is this elementary school?" I asked, rolling my eyes. Kendra was always silly when she got drunk.

"No, I'm serious. He came right up and knew we were roommates and he wanted to know if you were single."

"Did you tell him I'm out with a new man every night?" I kept up the false humor. I didn't know how much of what she was saying was true or how much she'd remember. "I have a very busy, very elite and exclusive waiting list, you know. Maybe I can fit him into my calendar in a decade or so from now. I'll have my people call his people."

She laugh-giggle-snorted and spoke with the cheer of the very drunk. "Told him you were single, but picky. Lived like a nun... mostly." She snickered. "You weren't a nun last week."

Her head fell back, eyes drooping. For a second, I thought she'd fallen asleep, but then she cracked one eye open. "Oh. He's...I remember now. I've seen him before. He's..."

I caught movement out of the corner of my eye and my heart gave a funny little skip. "...Right behind me."

Edward grinned apologetically. "I didn't mean to sneak up on you like that, I just wanted to make sure I caught you before you left."

"Um, thanks. Have a good night." I realized I sounded rude, but I had no idea what to say. It was his fault for catching me off guard. I was a writer, not into improv. I needed time to edit or I said stupid shit. Case in point.

"See, I told you!" Kendra called from the interior of the SUV. "She's picky!"

I shot her a glare even though she couldn't see me. "Ignore her, please."

He held out his hand. A small crowd of party guests went by and called out goodbyes to him, but he just waved without taking his eyes off me. Nervously, feeling silly as I stood there holding my borrowed shoes, I went to step off the curb and then stopped, stepping back into them. I wobbled a bit and he was there to steady me.

"It always amazes me how women can make it look so easy to walk in those things."

I shot him a look. "You clearly haven't seen me walking then."

"Oh, I have." He smiled slowly. "I'm still amazed."

Still holding onto my hand, he led me to the other side of the car and opened the door, helping me inside. He didn't let go. Kendra's eyes drifted closed and I sat there, not knowing what to do, sure I would screw everything up at any moment.

"I can't let you leave without you giving me your number." He finally released my hand, but he didn't close the door.

"Really?" I asked.

"Please." He gave me another charming smile. "I'll call tomorrow."

Chapter Six

In the blinding morning light, I realized the end of the night was probably a champagne-fueled dream. It was entirely possible that my over-active imagination made up the pleasant story in place of reality. In real life, Kendra had gotten sick halfway home and there had been nothing of the entire ride that had smacked of a fairytale. She was going to be pissed when she got the bill from the car company. And when she saw her purse.

The driver had helped me get Kendra upstairs and dump her on the couch. I'd made sure she was on her side, put a wastebasket next to the couch, and draped a blanket over her. All I remembered after that was turning the volume all the way up on my phone and falling asleep with my make-up still on. I was pretty sure I'd managed to get my dress off.

Now, as I pried my sticky eyes open, squinting against the bright sunlight streaming in through the window, I was certain I had imagined Edward. There was a good possibility that, when she regained consciousness, Kendra would tell me I'd spent the night talking to a palm tree or other inanimate object. I hadn't thought I'd been that drunk, but I must have been. How else could I make up something like the scenario that was running through my head?

Why would Prince Charming want my number?

I made it up. Okay. I know that so I can cut the disappointment short here and now.

Since I'd made it up, it wasn't like I was really expecting him to call, right? Of course, even if he *was* real, guys never really followed through on that kind of thing.

"No wonder I'm losing faith in love."

Of course, speaking out loud made me lose faith in life—it just about made my head fall off.

Oh, yeah. I'd had too much to drink last night.

Then my phone rang, proving that point yet again as the sound cut through my head like an icepick, an icepick driven through by a sledgehammer.

"Make it stop!" Kendra cried from the couch.

I rolled out of bed, ignored my churning stomach, and crawled across the floor, digging under the rejected outfits from last's night party preparations. Push-up bras, sequin dresses, costume jewelry, and a feather boa, but no phone.

"Make it stop!"

"I can't find it. It's like a drag show dressing room in here." I winced as the phone rang again. Why had I turned up the ringer volume?

Kendra knocked over a stack of bangle bracelets and grabbed my phone off the coffee table. She flung it towards my door and rolled over, groaning as she did so.

"Hello?" I said breathlessly, not bothering to look at the caller ID before answering.

"Good morning, Gabriella, this is Edward."

"You're kidding." I closed my eyes. I was such an idiot.

"Kind of an odd joke, don't you think?" He sounded amused.

"I thought I dreamt you. Not all of you, just the last part when you asked for my number." *Oh, man...Gabs, just shut up!* I shot Kendra a look. Was she awake? Coherent? She needed to be so she could stop me from saying stupid things.

"It was pretty late."

"Or early, depending on how you look at it," I said. "It's still early."

"Depending on how you look at it, I suppose."

Now I was sure he was trying not to laugh at me.

"It's one in the afternoon."

He let me take that in for a few seconds. I squinted at the clock, unable to read the time. *Oh, hell...I'm going blind!* I swatted a hand at the face of it and then fought a hysterical giggle when I realized there was a silk stocking covering it.

"One o'clock," I mumbled.

"One o'clock."

Head pounding, I crawled back to my bed and leaned against it.

"How about dinner tonight? Nothing fancy, just a local place I love. I'd like to spend more time with you."

I thought about the hours of recovery time dinner afforded me, plus the time I would need to shower and pull myself back together. I didn't let myself think about anything else. If I tried to figure out why he'd asked me out or what tonight meant, my head was going to explode. It felt like it might do that anyway.

"Dinner sounds great. Can we say eight o'clock?"

"Perfect," he said cheerfully. "I'll pick you up at eight."

Carefully, I lowered the phone back down and then my head. I needed a few more minutes. Just a few.

I ended up taking thirty and then had to all but crawl into the bathroom in a desperate search for something to help the headache. That done, I started chugging water and braced myself.

Next, I had to get Kendra up, because if I was going to be presentable by eight, I needed her help.

***

According to Kendra, a '*nothing fancy*' date was actually harder than finding something to wear to a clearly defined event. Kendra and I faced my closet for a good five minutes before either of us spoke.

"How many sport coats do you own?" she asked, a pained expression on her face.

"That was my Tina Fey phase." I sighed. "It's a

good look though. Maybe I should go with that tonight?"

"Gabriella, it's a date, not a business lunch. You have to show a little leg."

I sat down on the edge of my bed as Kendra started searching through the closet. I knew better than to get in her way when she was like this. Her expression was a varying range of disgust as she examined and tossed things aside. Some of the colors made her wince, a few textures made her shake her hand as if a snake had bitten her, and one blouse had her snickering for a good minute before she tossed it down and went back to mocking my wardrobe.

Scowling, I asked, "Are my clothes really that funny?"

"Yes." She smiled at me cheerfully as she pulled something out and studied it.

"That's it." I reached behind me and grabbed my phone. "I'm calling the date off."

"No!" She came striding to me, all leg and smiles and dumped an armful of possibilities on my bed. "You're going on your date and you're going to look beautiful."

"A date." I sighed, still clutching my phone. "I'm still kind of trying to wrap my head around that this is a date. Doesn't seem believable."

"What I can't believe is that I didn't get to meet this guy. He sounds delicious. Are you sure he works in the industry?"

"You met him twice, party girl," I said with a

grin. "Man, were you really that drunk?"

She grimaced. "I didn't eat much yesterday. Nervous, excited. That and the champagne..."

"Well, he seemed pretty popular at the party. A lot of people seemed to know who he was, but I'm not sure what he does."

"Well," said Kendra, "that's the perfect topic for a first date."

"You know I have been on dates before, right?"

She laughed and pulled me up to see the selection she'd laid out next to me on the bed. Somehow she'd found a black pencil skirt I'd forgotten I owned and she'd paired it with a bright green silk blouse and black sequined cardigan. My other choices included a blue sheath dress that made me look like someone's secretary or a cream-colored strapless dress with a lace overlay that she'd layered with a cropped denim jacket.

"Oooh, wait!" She practically squealed. "I have the perfect boots!"

I was already in the cream-colored dress when she brought in a pair of calf-high leather boots. The satin and lace of the dress dressed up the denim coat and the snug boots gave me just the right amount of country style to feel exactly like myself.

"Oh, Gabs, you look fantastic." She smiled at me in delight. Then she pointed a finger toward the bathroom. "Okay. Into the bathroom. Shower, hair, shave. You know the drill."

I rolled my eyes even as I eyed the clock. It was almost four. Picking out an outfit had taken nearly an hour. "Again...I've *been* on dates before."

But I followed the drill sergeant's orders and marched on.

***

Three hours later, I was giving myself a manicure. My toes were done. I'd even taken a forty minute nap on Kendra's advice. *You need more water, some juice and get some more ibuprofen in your system—it will help with the hangover.*

She'd done the same and it seemed to have helped both of us.

She was painting her toenails lime green.

Mine were a more sedate shade of coral, the same color as the glossy sheen I was applying to my nails.

"So how did you run into this guy?" she asked.

"He found me." I grinned up at her as I went to get more polish. "I thought he was looking to get the goods on you, but he asked me to dance and when he was done, he went over and talked to you. Apparently, he was pumping *you* for information about me instead of the other way around."

Kendra frowned. "You act like you never have guys showing interest, Gabs. I've had plenty of guys approach me about you before, and you know it. You're just...picky?"

Remembering Flynn, I decided I really needed to focus on my nails. "Not picky enough," I muttered.

"Hey."

I just shook my head.

She came over to me and sat down, absently fanning a hand back and forth. Sighing, I looked up at her. "Everybody runs into a bastard now and then," she said quietly.

"I know." I forced a smile. "I'm done thinking about him. Not like I'm going to see him anymore, right?"

I was going to focus on Edward now.

**

It was seven-fifty and I was in the bathroom, looping a couple strands of freshwater pearls around my neck. They'd been Kendra's grandmother's. A critical study in the mirror didn't set my nerves at ease any.

"You ready?"

"I'm *dressed*," I told Kendra. "Am I ready? Not sure."

The buzzer sounded and I jumped.

"Too bad." She grinned at me and went off to hit the intercom. "She'll be right down."

Then she grinned at me. "Go get 'em, girl. If he's hot and you plan on spending the night, just call me."

"No." I shook my head. "I did the whole get laid without strings thing, and I didn't like it." I didn't

70

add that it was just the afterwards part I didn't like. The sex itself had been amazing. "From here on out, it's about the romance."

She rolled her eyes, but didn't say anything as I left the apartment.

I'd already decided if Edward wasn't up to the task of wooing me, then I would be home and in bed with a steamy romance novel by ten o'clock.

Better a fictional man I could count on than a real one I couldn't. I wasn't in the mood to play around.

A grin spread across my face when I found him waiting at the door, holding it open for me.

"Thank you," I said.

Outside, his driver opened the town car door for us and I couldn't resist the impulse to ask, "So your last name is Charming, right? Like the prince?"

"Exactly." He said, grinning. "If my Cinderella likes Indian food. If not, then you're in the wrong carriage."

I smiled. "I love it." A weird sense of giddiness welled up inside me and I had to fight not to let any of it show on my face. I made do with a smile that hopefully didn't look too insanely happy.

The Lotus Chaat House was a narrow slot of a restaurant jammed in between an all-night bakery and a bodega that advertised the best churros in New York City. The town car slid up to the curve right in front of the jutting awning and the driver hopped out to open the door. I stepped out and looked up at the paint-peeling Taj Mahal sign with some trepidation. Not exactly what I'd expected, though it certainly wasn't fancy.

"Don't worry, just wait until you see inside," he promised.

The windows were steamed up, so I had to take Edward at his word and let him escort me inside. As soon as I stepped through the door, I knew he was right. The restaurant was magic. Beyond the heavenly scent of warm naan, the small alley-like restaurant was criss-crossed with so many strings of twinkle lights it glowed. The tiny starry bulbs were so thick across the ceiling that no other lights were used except small red glass jars with flickering candles on each of the tables. The golden-yellow walls were covered in shelves chock full of shining statuettes and lotus flowers.

"And the food's good too," Edward said, leaning close so he could speak in a low voice.

A smiling woman in a pink sari greeted Edward like an old friend before shooing us over to a table and clapping her hands at two waiters. If she hadn't been old enough to be his mother, I might've been jealous.

"It is so nice to see you, Mr. Edward, and you brought someone!" She beamed at me. "He used to eat alone. I told him I have three nieces that would be happy to join him, but he always declined. Now I know why—you are so beautiful!"

I was pleased to see Edward blush slightly at the sweet teasing. It made me feel better about my own red cheeks. Even though the space between the tables was minuscule, he still managed to pull my chair out for me. I sat down and wondered how exactly he had made a perfect cozy and romantic restaurant appear out of thin air. I could practically hear the romantic comedy love theme starting to play in the background.

A plate of naan and three small dishes of different chutneys were on the table when I managed to break out of my inner movie. Another smiling waiter uncorked a bottle of chardonnay and poured us each a glass.

"I took the liberty of pre-ordering some of my favorites," Edward said. He didn't seem to have noticed my little space-out. "But please pick anything off the menu you want."

I smiled. "Did you happen to order coconut curry? Maybe some lamb vindaloo?"

"I did."

"Then I'm a happy girl."

We clinked our wine glasses together and each took a drink. The alcohol warmed me, helping me to relax.

"Try the mango chutney," he said. "It's the perfect mix of sweet and spice."

He tore off a piece of the still warm bread and dipped it in the first small dish before leaning over and holding it out to me. I savored the sting of spices mellowed by the bright sugary taste of mango, the flavors bursting across my taste buds as I took a bite of the bread he'd offered.

His eyes warmed as I licked the crumbs from my

lips and my heart kicked up.

"Tell me what you do during the day, Prince Charming," I asked.

"I wear a suit and a tie and stand in an office wishing I was here with you."

I felt my cheeks turn pink and made a mental note to write that line down when I got home. It should've made me roll my eyes, but there was no doubting his sincerity.

"So, do you love your work?" As much as I liked what he'd said, I wanted to know more about him.

"I do," he admitted. "It's the family business so it sort of runs itself. I'm actually more of a referee between the shareholders, but I'm happy. How about you?"

"Well, I'm leagues away from anything to do with shareholders," I said. "I'm an assistant to a screenwriter. Or, as I like to call it, a personal slave to a psycho." I laughed, but I was only half-joking. My boss was a nightmare.

"Exciting then?"

"Oh, yes," I agreed. "I never know if it's going to be a quiet day fetching coffee or I'll be spending an hour on the phone searching for double-chocolate strawberry expresso beans."

He laughed. "That does sound exciting. Are those even a real thing?"

I shrugged and took a drink. "I don't know. I'm still searching for them."

We both laughed and I realized I was seriously considering transitioning into a heavily censored version of my foray into hand modeling when a plate of samosas arrived and we both eyed them hungrily. I watched him crunch into the flaky crust and close his eyes as he chewed the mouth-watering mix of spiced ground beef and peas. With his eyes closed, I was able to get a good look at him without him knowing.

He was wearing a navy blue suit, but this time without a tie and, in the twinkling glow of the restaurant, he looked relaxed and happy. I noticed his light brown hair was sun-streaked and the open collar of his shirt showed a muscular and tan chest. His eyes opened and I turned my attention to my own plate.

"You seem like the sporty type. What do you do for fun?" I asked, trying to get my mind off of those broad shoulders.

"Promise not to judge?"

I grinned. "Only if you give me the last samosa."

"Deal." He pushed the small plate across the table. "Polo."

"You mean with the game thingy with the horses?"

"That's the one."

He sipped his wine and watched me, as if my reaction to his revelation was important. I liked that he cared what I thought, although I wasn't sure why he was concerned about what I'd think of a game.

"Sounds like fun," I said and he relaxed.

The main dishes arrived, steaming up the small window above our table, and Edward ordered another bottle of wine. We skipped separate plates and shared bites from each savory dish, rolling our eyes and moaning at each tantalizing taste. Our conversation veered off into favorite books we read in childhood and we laughed over our shared secret love of science fiction.

"I thought I was the only one that carried a towel around my backyard and waited to hitchhike on passing spaceships," I said.

"Are you kidding? I got a telescope just to look for rides out into the galaxy."

When we finished, we both tipped back in our chairs. I looked down at the table, startled by the sheer volume of food we'd consumed. It was probably a good thing I'd skipped the narrow pencil skirt.

"Do you want to take a walk?" Edward asked.

"I'd better or you'll have to roll me home." I smiled.

He paid the bill without letting me argue about splitting it and we strolled down the block where he signaled to his driver to move on. The car slowly drifted away and we turned the corner. I saw Washington Square a few blocks away and Edward slipped an arm around my waist as we walked towards it. His hand rested on my hip, a warm brand. *We're together,* that touch said. I liked it.

We passed several wide gallery windows where New York's socialites were fawning over new artists. I stopped in front of one white-walled gallery displaying black and white photographs. They reminded me of Flynn. I tried to swallow the ache that rose in my chest as I remembered the look in his eyes as he'd aimed the camera held such passion, so focused, so intent.

Stop it.

I wanted to be there, leaning against Edward with his arm around my waist, but my mind suddenly fixed on Flynn, wondering where in the world he was at that moment.

Probably French-kissing some silly waitress in Paris or seducing a young senorita in Spain, I thought and tried to shake him from my head.

"Everything alright?" Edward asked, his tone concerned.

"I'm fine," I said, dragging my thoughts away from the images. I put my head on his shoulder.

The farther we got from the gallery, the easier it was to put Flynn out of my head, the easier it was to focus on the man next to me. It was so easy being with him. Just walking in the warmth of the night— everything felt easy. "Maybe you should pinch me. Is it just me or is this date going really well?"

Edward stopped me at the edge of the park and turned me so we were facing each other. When I didn't look up, too focused on trying to remember how to breathe, he reached out and tipped my chin up. His pale eyes studied me for a moment before he leaned close and softly grazed his lips across mine. The caress left me sighing and I raised myself up on tiptoe to return the light kiss. He slid his hands down to the small of my back and pulled me close.

This time, when his mouth came down on mine, the pressure made my lips part so he could deepen the kiss. He cradled my head with one hand and used the other to arch my back, lifting me up deeper into the kiss.

It was intense, sweet and poignantly romantic. My heart began to race as his mouth took mine. I felt like someone from a movie and a shiver of pleasure ran down my spine.

When he slowly broke away, my head was spinning and his hands gripped my waist almost convulsively, as if he was fighting the urge to kiss me—and more.

His eyes locked on mine, brighter blue from the heat of the moment. Still holding me around the waist, he signaled for the nearby town car with one hand. I held my breath, not sure how to respond to the invitation I assumed was coming next. I'd wanted romance and not just sex, but I couldn't deny how much I wanted him right now.

"I'd say it went very well, Gabriella." He lifted a hand and caressed my cheek. "Paul will take you home. I'm a little warm so I think I'll walk."

"Goodnight?" I whispered and stared at him. Was he serious?

He pulled me tightly to him again and we both melted into another kiss. Then I felt his arms tense and press me back, as if he didn't trust himself to kiss me any longer.

"Can I see you tomorrow night?" he asked, his voice a bit breathless. "I have tickets to the theater.

Please?"

"Sure thing, Mr. Charming," I said as I climbed into the car. This date was going to keep me for a while.

***

When Kendra came home late Sunday morning, she stumbled over a wide box in our narrow hallway. "Oh, hey now...just *what* do we have here, Gabs? You picked up a secret admirer or what?"

"You're one to talk." I scowled at her. "Where have you been, Ms. Thing?"

"Obviously out with a lower class of guy. Where's *my* giant post first date present?" she asked with a grin.

Before I could reach for it, she tore open the card and read it out loud.

"Darling Gabriella. Last night was a dream. My fairy godmother saw this and thought of you. I can't wait to see you in it tonight. In anticipation, Prince Charming."

She handed over the card as she gushed, "Damn, Gabs, seems you've cast a spell with all your talk of love and romance."

I pushed Kendra out of the way and shimmied open the box lid. Inside was a long dress in the deepest lapis lazuli blue. The plunging neckline touched a satin empire waist before the dress undulated in soft waves to the floor.

"Wow," Kendra breathed. "Wait! I have the perfect shoes to match!"

***

With my own fairy godmother providing me with pale gold, sparkling shoes, I felt like Cinderella that night as I carefully swept down our front steps in my elegant gown. Edward was waiting, a broad smile stretching across his face as he escorted me to the town car where Paul was waiting with the door open. I smiled at the driver and he tipped his hat in return.

"So where are we off to?" I asked as we settled into the back seat.

"I have two tickets to see the most popular show on Broadway," he said.

I studied him for a moment. "You have no idea what the show is called, do you?"

"No." He laughed. "Do you know what show everyone's been talking about?"

"Sorry. Unless it's reality TV, my friends have nothing to say, and I tend to stick with what's on the small screen for work."

"Well, luckily the marquee should be big enough for us to figure it out before we walk in," he said. "And if we don't, it'll be a pleasant surprise."

When Paul, our driver, pulled up in front of the theater, I looked up at the marquee and couldn't help myself. "Oooh, I always wanted to see that!"

His gaze followed mine and he smiled. We were in for a spectacular rendition of Cleopatra's love story.

It was everything I could've dreamed it would be. Completely enchanted by the spellbinding production, we held hands through the entire show. Despite the electricity flowing between us, neither of us looked away from the stage.

During intermission, Edward kept seeing people he knew. I half expected him to deposit me in the corner with a drink while he greeted his friends. After all, I wasn't one of them.

Instead, he kept my arm tucked in the crook of his elbow and introduced me to everyone we saw. I felt like I was walking in a dream.

"Edward, I didn't know you were seeing anyone." A white-haired woman in an oversized ruby necklace looked down her nose at me. "I thought perhaps you were seeing Talia's daughter."

"Allison, this is Gabriella."

Kendra often added phrases like "she's a really talented writer" in a way that made me feel uncomfortable. She'd never really read anything I'd written so the white lie made me feel like I was not enough on my own.

Edward, on the other hand, simply introduced me as me and left it at that, like I was enough to be a singular name. He then steered me away with a confidence that said any other information was none of the obvious gossip's business.

"People seem very interested in your dating life,"

I said once we were out of earshot of his admirers.

"My mother is a patron here. These are actually tickets she gave me."

I considered the question. "And were you supposed to bring Talia's daughter?"

"Perhaps," he said with a smile. "But then again I got lucky and you said yes."

The house lights blinked and we returned to our seat. The rest of the show was romantic and tragic, just as I'd known it would be. We held hands again despite the obvious disapproval of Mrs. Allison Whitehair who was watching from her private box.

"Do you think she's going to tattle on you?" I whispered, barely suppressing a laugh.

"Probably." His breath tickled my ear.

"Will your mother be angry?" I asked, honestly curious.

"She could be."

He turned to me with a mischievous smile. "If that's the case, I should give her a reason to really be upset." Then, without waiting another moment, he pulled me into a dramatic kiss. It started off theatrically and ended with a surprising amount of heat. When he set me back in my seat, an entire song had gone by and my heart felt like it was going to burst from my chest. I was breathless, my heart was racing and I had to consciously uncurl my hands from his arms.

The white-haired gossip might not have enjoyed the extra performance, but I didn't care. The moment his lips had parted mine, I hadn't been aware of anything but him. Not the people, the play, the music. Only the feel of his mouth moving against mine, the heat of his hands...

When the show was over, Paul was waiting outside with the door already open, as if he'd known we'd want to leave quickly. Once inside the car, Edward gathered me in close and three blocks went by before we surfaced from an even more thorough and intense kiss. My entire body was throbbing, my nipples hard and tight, aching against the strapless bra.

The pulsing between my legs was profound and it took all of my self-control to keep from grinding against him.

"We have reservations," he said.

"Delicious." I ran my fingers through his hair, wanting to see what it looked like mussed rather than professionally styled.

"Or we could send Paul for take-out."

Hell, yes. I nodded and with a quick rap on the partition, Edward took us away from the glitz and glamour of downtown. When I looked out the window a few minutes later, my jaw dropped.

Living in New York City, it was easy to forget that some neighborhoods had trees. Not just the skinny little trees that sat in open circles in the concrete, but big trees with wide spreading branches. Trees that arched up and over the street. Streets that were lined with private homes bigger than my entire apartment building.

When we drove through tall wrought-iron gates

to a palatial limestone mansion, I started to feel like a fairytale character again. I actually lost a golden heel on his expansive front steps. Running back to grab it, I realized I had not hallucinated. His house had not one but two turrets. I felt myself quickly going from feeling like I was in a fairytale to feeling completely out of place.

"You live in a castle?" I asked as he came back down to my side.

"It's only temporary," he said, his tone almost dismissive. "It's a family home. I stay here while my own place is being remodeled."

Edward must have sensed my sudden hesitation as he gave my hand a slight squeeze. "Don't worry. We are all alone. My family only uses this place as a vacation home in the summer."

With that said, Edward pulled me through the echoing foyer and into the snug warmth of a side room. I didn't see much of the house as we went, too caught up in the feel of his hands on me, but I didn't care. If it was between the house and the man, I knew which one I was choosing.

"This is my favorite room in the house." He wrapped his arms around me from behind and nuzzled the spot under my ear. "We can relax here unless you want a tour?"

I shook my head, reluctantly stepping away from him. I needed a brief moment to gather myself and I took it by settling down on the buttery tan leather couch. A small fire flickered on the stone hearth and I wondered if he'd had someone start it for him.

While I was wondering, Edward poured two crystal cut glasses of whiskey and handed me one before stretching out on the Persian rug in front of me. I tousled his light brown hair and we watched the fire as we sipped.

Somewhere in the cavernous foyer, a grandfather clock chimed and I wondered when I was going to turn into a pumpkin. Surely this was too much of a dream to last long. But even as minutes ticked by, Edward was still the same easy conversationalist with a sweet smile and a bright sense of humor. The whiskey and fire started to warm me inside and out and I relaxed.

As we talked about *Cleopatra* and laughed about our kiss in the theater, the heat between us began to build again. With his eyes on my face, he wrapped his fingers around my ankle. I stretched out my leg and waited to see what he was going to do. My breathing quickened as he slid his hand up my calf. He sat up, shifting his weight so that he could move his hand under my skirt, leaving fire burning across my knee and thigh. The hem dragged up along with his exploring hand, and he leaned down, kissing the skin he exposed. His eyes met mine as he paused above my knee, wordlessly asking for permission. I answered by lying back on the couch.

He trailed his mouth up my inner thigh and grazed the heat between my legs. I moaned as I ran both my hands through his hair. My back arched when he wet the thin fabric of my lace underwear with a long heavy lick of his tongue and he chuckled, a deep, manly sound that made my insides twist. He leaned back, one long finger pulling aside the crotch of my panties to gain better access.

"Ah!" I cried out as his tongue delved between my folds.

He worked over my clit before dancing down to my entrance, each pass making my legs tremble. When he took my clit between his teeth and lightly tugged, I keened, the sound coming from a place deep inside me. He slowly pushed one finger inside me, twisting his wrist as he did so and I tensed, feeling an orgasm building inside me.

He didn't push me immediately over, instead taking his time to bring up slowly and when I came, it was with a harsh, desperate cry. My fingers tightened in his hair and I gasped out his name as he gave my clit another gentle tug with his teeth.

I came down slowly, my body shuddering as he continued to tease me. Unable to take it, I pulled on his head, drawing him up onto the couch to kiss me. The deep, exploring thrusts of his tongue were mirrored by the rubbing press of his growing hardness, and I could taste myself on his lips and tongue.

"I need you," he said roughly. "Can I...?"

"Do you even have to ask?" I arched myself closer, so desperate now that I might have cried if he'd tried to pull away.

Edward broke away and got to his feet. He made short work of his shirt and then held out his hand.

I took it and let him help me to my feet. His

hands slid over my shoulders, taking the straps of my dress with them.

"You know," he said quietly. "The first time I saw this dress, I knew I wanted to see you in it." He reached around and slowly pulled down the zipper. "And then I wanted to take you out of it."

The words left me trembling even more and I stared at him, blushing even as I smiled while the dress dropped to the floor. It pooled around my bare feet and for a moment, Edward just stared at me. I went to take my bra off, but he caught my hands, guiding them to my sides and then he took over the task, opening the front catch.

I moaned when he cupped my breasts in his hands, his thumbs circling around my nipples. They were aching and tight and each touch felt so good. Arching into his touch, I reached out and gripped his shoulders.

Skilled hands slid down my ribcage to my hips and he hooked his fingers in the waistband of my panties. With his eyes blazing, he went to his knees and took my panties with him. I stepped out of them, balancing myself with my hands on his shoulders. He looked up at me and kissed the inside of my thigh before standing.

"My turn." He took off his pants, the movements quick, but not rushed. I had a moment to admire the way his black boxer briefs hugged his body and then they were joining the pants.

His cock was rigid and my pussy throbbed, a clenching need settling deep inside at the sight of him. He drew me to him with both hands, running them down my bare back as we kissed and let our naked bodies touch. The slow tickling circles he traced on my ass made me moan. He answered with a deep guttural sigh before lowering me to the rug.

He took a brief moment to roll on a condom and then our bodies joined in one silky push and I curled my knees up on either side of his hips in pure pleasure. He moved slowly, circling before drawing out and then pressing back deep into the center of me. His lips and tongue made trails across my collarbone and breasts, little licks of fire before he fastened his mouth around my nipple. He sucked on it hard, sending an almost painful jolt straight through to my core. He waited as my climax came closer, my hands opening and closing on his back, urging him forward. I was right at the edge and I felt his body tighten.

"Are you ready?" he asked through gritted teeth. I could see the strain on his face.

I nodded. "Please."

He shifted his hips as he thrust into me, hitting that spot inside me even as the base of his cock pressed against my clit. I called out his name, wrapping my legs around him to hold him as close as possible as his orgasm joined mine. Our bodies rocked together, drawing out every possible moment of exquisite pleasure.

Even after we came apart, we lay there in front of the fire until it was nothing but winking embers. I was curled up against him, both of us partially covered by a blanket he'd pulled from the couch.

The heat left me drowsy and languid, but I wouldn't let myself sleep. I didn't want to miss a moment of this. Every so often, he tipped the whiskey glass to my lips and we drank together in long, lingering kisses.

When the ivory-plated clock chimed two, I finally stood up. I needed to leave or I wouldn't make myself leave at all.

He sent a quick message with his phone before pulling on his pants.

"You could stay if you wanted to," he told me as I dressed.

I just shook my head as I picked up my shoes. We paused at the door and he kissed me again.

"Stay," he murmured.

"Never before the third date." I had to harden my reserve though.

He groaned, although it was a playful sound. He opened the door and escorted me down the steps. The town car was waiting with the door open. He must have sent Paul a message.

He caught my hand before I got into the car. "What are you doing Tuesday?"

Chapter Seven

"You're going out with him again?"

I rolled my eyes at the disapproval in her voice. "I know it seems a little crazy, Kendra, but he's wonderful. You'd like him."

She slapped butter on the toast and left it on the counter untouched. Her light green eyes were flashing. "You don't even know his last name and you're seeing an awful lot of him."

"You know," I said mildly. "For someone who came home at three in the morning on a Monday night, wait, Tuesday morning, you sound awfully judgmental."

Kendra gnashed into her slice of toast and tossed the other one down the counter at me. We ate in silence as the coffee finished brewing. I poured her a cup and turned to get the milk. I didn't like arguing with her, but I was a little tired of her double standards. I'd never said anything about her dating habits.

"He's totally distracted you from getting a job,"

she said.

"That's not true. He's distracting me from the hell that is my job. I'm happy, K. Can I just be happy for a week?"

She took the coffee and kissed my cheek. "Fine. You can be happy until rent is due again."

I was still a little annoyed, but I didn't want to fight anymore. "You don't know. Maybe Edward is just dating me because he can sense I'm the world's next top hand model." I said, trying to lighten the mood.

I knew she was stressing over the rent. I was, too. We'd put in another call about the landlord issue, but nobody had returned our call and if we didn't hear from somebody soon, we were either going to have to pay the insane amount that was being asked or leave. It pissed me off because we knew we were being jerked around, but unless we could get somebody to talk to us, what were we supposed to do?

She grumbled under her breath and left to go shower and pack up. She had a photo shoot that was supposed to last most of the day and I needed to get to work too.

Just a couple of hours and I'd see Edward again. After a crazy week, I needed it.

***

Psycho-boss was even more psycho than

normal. Even the people who normally fawned over her and kissed her psycho-boss ass were steering clear of her and when she left for lunch, I took my shot at escape, more than happy to head to my lunch date with Edward.

Instead of a restaurant, however, he'd asked me to meet him at Bethesda Fountain in Central Park. I smiled as I saw him coming towards me. He'd left his tie and suit coat in the car, but it was obvious he was coming straight from work. He lifted me up into a joyous kiss before he rolled up his sleeves and threaded my arm through his. We weaved through the tourists taking pictures and wandered further into the park.

"How's work?" I asked.

"Same old. I have a big meeting this afternoon so I can't stay too long."

I tried not to feel too disappointed. "Then you better kiss me again." I dragged him off the path and leaned up against an oak tree, pulling him towards me. He leaned into me and I wrapped my arms around his neck before our lips met again. The kiss was far too brief for my taste.

"Mmm," he murmured against my neck. "I'm hungry."

Teasingly, I said, "But you said you don't have much time...and we can't do *that* here."

He chuckled and pulled away. "I meant food. Come on."

"Since we don't have much time, what do you suggest? Hot dog vendor?" I asked, looking around.

The carts were everywhere.

"I have a better idea." He led me around the tree to a clearing I hadn't seen until that moment.

Paul waved to us from a blanket on an open spot on the grass. He'd spread out a perfect picnic lunch in view of the lake.

"Wow." I breathed out a happy sigh. "That's much better than a vendor."

Once we settled onto the wool blanket, he opened the wine, handed it to Edward, and left us alone.

"You don't want to talk about work and you have a driver who also delivers picnics." I sipped my wine for a moment and then looked up at Edward, lowering my voice to a conspiratorial whisper. "Are you Batman?"

Edward chuckled. "More like Batman's dutiful son who does all the boring work of keeping a family business afloat."

"Ah, you're right. The more you say 'family business' the more I know you must be in the mob." I grinned at him.

"Again, far more exciting than what I do."

He clinked his wine glass against mine and spread a bite of soft cheese on a chunk of baguette.

"Besides, I'd rather hear about your world."

"You mean the glamorous world of writing pages for peanuts? The one where I once contemplated using toilet paper for a coffee filter because, after my rent was paid, I couldn't afford to buy even the cheap ones?"

"Yes, that one," Edward said with a smile. "The one where you love the actual work despite everything else. Including toilet paper coffee."

He popped a bite of salami in my mouth and I sucked his fingers before savoring the salty bite. He licked his lips and moved in closer. Feeling something like Cleopatra, I took a taste of briny olive from his fingers. He rubbed the other half along my lower lip and then bent to kiss its taste from my mouth. I could get used to eating this way.

The next few minutes passed in a lazy, sensual silence and I felt the stress of the morning passing away.

"I have to go soon, but please say we can meet for dinner." Edward brushed his fingers across my cheek as he spoke.

"Yes, please," I said.

"This doesn't bother you?"

"What?" I gave him a puzzled look.

"I know I'm moving us a little fast, but I can't help it. If I didn't have this meeting I would want to spend the whole day with you." There wasn't a trace of insincerity in his voice.

"I don't understand why people think all relationships follow the same timeline," I said. "Some start fast and some take years to develop."

Without meaning to, my mind jumped to the firework blast of Flynn. I had to remind myself it was a fling, not a relationship. No matter how much I tried to stop it, he kept coming to mind and the flash of him always made my heart thump. *Stop it*, I told myself, adding in a mental kick in the ass.

Those two were on total opposite ends of the spectrum.

On the good side was Edward, sitting next to me on the blanket. He whispered questions in my ear about the people we saw in the park and we sipped our wine and laughed as I made up back-stories. The good was us feeding each other creamy bites of Brie cheese and sweet red grapes in between shared smiles, and it would've been just as good if the food had been cheap cheddar and crackers.

The bad was the burst of heat I felt when a man walked by with a camera. My cheeks flared as I remembered the teasing pressure of Flynn's fingers inside me, the flood of pleasure as he'd slowly pulled them out and rubbed me until I'd panted. How he'd felt filling me. The bad was the way he'd jerked his head to the bathroom, telling me I could clean up, collect my cash and get out, thanks, bye. The embarrassment of it *still* stung.

"Don't let the wine go to your head," Edward said, mistaking the pink in my cheeks for something else.

I wasn't about to correct him. "I'm not the one that has a meeting to go to." I reminded him.

"Speaking of that." He sighed. "I have to go. Dinner? Tonight?"

"Yes and yes."

"Meet me at The Lotus?" he asked. "I'll send Paul to pick you up."

I agreed and we went our separate ways. I

picked up my pace, trying to outrun the remembered passion with Flynn.

I'd just had a lovely picnic with Edward and we'd spent the other night together, perfect, romantic and sexy. He'd walked me to the door, asked me, wistfully, if I could spend the night. Then he had kissed me until my toes curled.

Yet my body warmed at the thought of Flynn putting down his camera with lust bright in his dark blue eyes.

I shook my head and walked faster. For once, I hoped work could keep me too busy to think.

***

Later that night, Edward stepped out of a taxi and joined me under the Taj Mahal crowned awning. He looked rumpled and tired, still in the same suit from earlier. Still, he gave me a smile and a kiss.

"How about take out?" I asked.

He gave me a grateful look. "You are a dream come true."

He had Paul take our order and we lounged in the town car while we waited.

"Work was that bad, huh?" I asked.

"Not work, family. Sometimes it's like trapping wild dogs in a room. You're trying to feed them, be nice to them, and all they do is snarl and nip."

"Your meeting was with your family?" I asked.

"They're board members so I have to include

97

them. We even had to wait for one to conference call from Amsterdam. Impossible. Just one of the reasons no one else will take the job." He craned his head on the back of the seat and gave me a tired smile. "Tell me about your day, Gabriella."

I shrugged and said, "What do you want to hear? About psycho-boss's latest rampage?"

His eyes lit with humor. "Yes."

So I told him, happy to see some of the strain leaving his eyes.

We made small talk until we got to Edward's house. Once there, I spread the Indian food out on the sideboard in his study while he started a fire. The air wasn't cold, but we both enjoyed the cozy fireplace. I piled up two plates and he poured two glasses of wine. We sat side by side on the floor and dug in. I wanted to ask him more about work, but he sidestepped it and we ended up arguing about the best movies of the eighties.

"I love this," he said suddenly.

"What?" I asked, surprised. "Debating bad movies?"

"No," he said with a smile. "I love the fact that we can sit here for an entire meal without music, television, or other people and there's never an awkward silence."

I paused for as long as I could before I asked, "You mean like that one?"

He rolled his eyes. "I'm serious, Gabriella, I don't think I've ever dated someone who was such a perfect match."

He leaned over and kissed me, a soft kiss at first. A soft kiss that quickly became something filled with fire and passion. It wasn't hurried though. This time, he slowly undressed me, leaving a trail of searing kisses after each removed article of clothing. When I was completely naked, he lifted me onto the couch to straddle his lap. With his arms around my waist, he rocked me up and down against his dress pants until we were both wet from my arousal and his cock was straining against his zipper. Teasing my nipples with his tongue, he fumbled with his pants.

"Darling," he gasped. "Wait, I need..."

"I'm on the pill." I reached down to cup his hardness through his pants. "And I'm clean." I locked eyes with him. "Are we good?"

He nodded wordlessly, then groaned as I freed his cock from its confines. I slipped down on him, turned on by the texture of his clothes against my bare body. It heightened the slick skin on skin where our bodies joined and his hands guided me. "That's it," he murmured, bringing one hand up to cup my breast. "Harder...faster..."

He threw his head back, the hand at my breasts almost painful.

His cock swelled and I shuddered, feeling myself locking down around him, tightening as my orgasm moved closer.

I whimpered and fell forward, the angle changing and now each movement had me rubbing my clitoris against him and it was so, *so* good. "Come for me, Gabriella," he said against my neck, scraping his teeth against my skin.

His thumb circled my nipple and I tensed.

Inside me, the head of his cock passed over my G-spot and I broke, coming around him hard and fast. As though he'd been waiting for just that, he started to drive up into me, each movement quicker and rougher than before.

Three strokes later and he was right there with me, groaning out my name as he climaxed.

Long, breathless moments passed, his hands smoothing up and down my back. I smiled dreamily against his chest when I heard the ragged sound of his heartbeat, slamming in a rhythm that echoed mine.

"Please tell me you can stay tonight."

"Hmmm..." I turned my face into his neck. "It *is* the third date."

"That's a yes?" His arm tightened around my waist.

"Yes."

***

The next morning, I woke up in Edward's upstairs master suite.

I was alone in the king-sized bed and for one panicked moment, I froze. Then I heard the shower running and the tension drained away.

Smiling that giddy smile that tried so often to overtake me, I stretched and turned my head, following the sound of splashing water until I saw the closed door. We definitely weren't taking things slow, but everything felt so comfortable, so right.

We liked the same foods, laughed at the same television shows, loved the same bad science fiction, and had the same ideas of what constituted a perfect day. Though, as the sunlight streamed into his inner sanctum, I realized there was one giant divide between us. I shifted uneasily.

He was rich. Not just hard-working, the right kind of career rich, but family legacy money rich. I may not have known who his family was, but there was no doubt about it. The master suite not only had a fireplace, it had a family crest engraved above it.

The sound of water cut off and I sat up, looking around nervously for something to put on. I didn't quite manage to come up with anything before the bathroom door opened and Edward appeared in the opening, smiling at me.

"You're awake. Good morning, gorgeous."

"Hmmm. I was lazing about for a few more minutes." I glanced down and watched as a bead of water slid down his chest.

"Laze away." He smiled at me. "In fact, Paul's going to run me in to the office. I'll have breakfast sent up and by the time you've eaten, he'll be back. When you're ready, he'll drive you to work."

Ah yes, work. Slaving away for a menial wage while desperately hoping that my talent would one day be recognized. The perfect thing to remind me of how different our lives were.

He leaned down to kiss me as someone knocked on the door. His lips brushed against mine and then he called for whoever it was to enter. A moment later, a maid brought in a silver breakfast tray. She gave him a polite nod, but didn't even look at me as she left the tray on the dresser. He thanked her and followed her out, pausing to blow me a kiss at the door.

Poached eggs with salmon, fresh bread lightly toasted, and a French press of heavenly strong coffee all tempted me from the foot of the bed, but first I reached for my phone.

"Okay. This is killing me...I still can't get him to tell me his last name." I eyed the crest, something elegant and Old World looking and shook my head. "He says he's not Batman, but that's all I can get out of him."

"Are you calling me from his bed?"

Of course that would be her first question. "Yes. He's left me here with a luxury breakfast that was delivered by a maid. When I'm done, a car will take me to work."

"Think you can get some coffee filters while you have access to a chauffeur? We're out. Have you ever tried the bodega's coffee? I think it may actually be muddy water they warm up and throw sugar in."

"You bought their coffee?"

"It was cheaper than the filters. So do you have a plan to figure out what he's hiding?"

"I do," I said, pouring fragrant coffee into a delicate China cup. "I'm going to call in late with some excuse and then tell the driver I'm supposed to meet Edward at his office. Boom, I find out what this family business is and why he's hiding his last name."

"Just the fact that he won't tell you his last name should be a red flag," Kendra said.

I sighed. "Yes, and then I think of the romantic dates, the great conversations, and the oh-so-sweet sex. Really, what's in a name?"

"Seriously, Juliet? You do remember how that whole 'what's in a name' thing worked for her and her boy?"

I scowled at the phone.

She continued, "Well, text me if your office surprise doesn't work. Then bring him to Tony's so I can meet him. Someone better assess if he's a knight in shining armor or a thinly veiled psycho-killer."

"Ah, Tony's Pizza," I said. "Always the perfect Plan B."

Paul was dozing in the front seat of the town car when the maid opened the front door for me twenty minutes later. She coughed loudly and he jolted awake and jumped out to open the car door. I smiled, wondering how much sleep the poor guy had gotten in the past few days. Edward and I had to have been running him ragged.

"Where to, Ms. Gabriella?"

"Edward told me to meet him at his office." I tried to sound breezy and casual. Whether or not he believed me, Paul nodded and started the car.

We headed straight into Manhattan. Paul had

fierce driving skills. He could give any New York cabbie a run for his money. He navigated snarled lanes of traffic, using his Bluetooth to send messages on his cellphone.

By the time we made it to the curb outside a giant building, I was both terrified and impressed. Then I saw where we were and all of the blood drained from my face. It had to be a mistake.

"The Bouvier Building?" I asked faintly.

Before Paul could answer, the door opened and Edward leaned in.

"Going my way?" His smile said he wasn't mad that I'd just showed up at his job unannounced. Paul must have sent him a message.

I swallowed and fought to keep from looking at the building behind him. "No fair..." I managed a weak smile. "I was just on my way to surprise you."

"Well, it's a little early for lunch, but I know a great place up the Hudson River that serves life-saving Bloody Marys. What do you say?"

Before I could answer, he got in the car and I had to swallow my frown. Paul screeched away from the curb before I even got to ask which gargantuan office building housed Edward's mysterious family business. I hoped it wasn't the same one where I'd met Flynn.

It was time for Plan B. Thinking quickly, I grinned up at him. "I'd say a Bloody Mary sounds delicious, but I already have a date."

"I thought you said you were surprising me." He sounded puzzled but not suspicious.

104

"Surprise!" I said weakly. "We're having lunch with my roommate, Kendra. Tony's Pizza, Paul."

Before Edward could respond, I gave Paul the address and he swerved across two lanes to make the turn. I smiled brightly at Edward as I discreetly texted Kendra the words 'Plan B'.

We rode in silence for a few minutes before Edward started asking about my childhood in Tennessee. His honest inquiries softened me up and by the time we reached Tony's Pizza, I had almost forgotten what had me so concerned.

Kendra, however, hadn't. She was waiting outside and strode up to Edward as soon as he got out of the car, a familiar expression on her face. She was in full-on mama bear mode, ready to protect me from anyone who might hurt me.

"Hello. I'm Gabriella's roommate, Kendra. Kendra Facet." She stuck out her hand.

He took it with a smile. "Nice to meet you, I'm Edward."

"Sorry, Edward," she said. "I didn't catch your last name."

"Don't worry." He smiled. "Just Edward is fine."

Kendra gave me a dire glance over his shoulder before speaking to him again. "You know, you look very familiar to me."

"That's not surprising. We met at the big Bouvier party. The night I met Gabriella."

He slipped an arm around my waist and kissed my temple.

"Come on, my darlings," I said. Time to move

from straight interrogation to polite lunch conversation. "Pizza's on me."

Chapter Eight

I never thought eating a slice of pizza at Tony's could be awkward. It was home base for after-debauchery food and I had seen everything from a drunken cello performance to a bout of mistaken identity happen in that small sliver of a restaurant.

Nothing had left a bad taste in my mouth until lunch with Kendra and Edward.

He was secretive, deftly fielding questions to avoid having to answer, and she was understandably suspicious. Kendra was sure they had met before the party and she kept squinting at him as if recognition was just a hard stare away. Edward looked terribly out of place in the pizza-by-the-slice place and spent an almost rude amount of time dabbing the grease off his plain cheese, yet another glaring example of how far apart our worlds were.

Together, they made me so nervous I tried to pitch them some script material and chattered away about the foibles of subway-riders non-stop.

Needless to say, halfway through that, Edward told me he had to get back to work, which meant I had to pretend that I needed to go too. He kissed me awkwardly in front of Kendra and told me the next few days were full of meetings. I told him I had a sit-down with a producer interested in a pilot script and then had to make up a television show on the spot. I titled it *Slice of Life* and was pretty sure he realized I'd lied.

When he walked out the door, I was certain I'd never see him again, and the thought hurt me more than I'd thought possible.

***

"He still hasn't called?" Kendra asked me three days later.

"Shh, I have two more pages to finish for a deadline."

"Gabs, I can see that you're writing a complaint about cereal." She pulled my laptop away from me. "I didn't mean to kill your whole relationship, I just wanted to make sure he was being honest with you."

I wanted to snap at her that it was all her fault for making me doubt him, but had to bite my tongue because I knew she'd just been looking out for me. I knew there was something he wasn't telling me about his family and, while I was hoping it was just that he seriously disliked them, his omissions were a little bothersome.

Sighing, I looked up at her. "He wasn't being honest with me. But..." I shrugged. "We haven't been dating long enough for me to know his address much less his life story."

Although I did sleep *with him...at his home. I slept with the guy. But I didn't know his last name.*

It was enough to leave me with a funny feeling in my gut and I knew Kendra hadn't been entirely off-base. I had to set aside my frustration with her. I knew that.

I gave her a wan smile.

"Maybe it's for the best, it was moving way too fast." If I said it enough, I'd believe it, right? Besides, she was my friend and friendship came first.

"No, you were right," she said, her face bleak. "It wasn't moving too fast, it was moving exactly how you wanted it to. And I screwed it up."

"I think all three of us did." I went back to staring at my laptop. "If he'd just told me who he is...if I hadn't stressed so much..."

"If *I* hadn't stressed *you* so much," Kendra added sourly.

I grinned at her. "Yeah, that. If he's just going to let it go because he can't understand why I wanted to know more about him..." I shrugged. "What can I do?"

"Still." She bent down behind me and hugged me. "I'm sorry, Gabs."

I was hoping her apology would turn into another invite out for free drinks and catered snacks since I could really use some alcohol, but my phone rang.

My heart flipped when I saw the name on the

caller ID.

I sucked in a breath and showed it to Kendra.

Her eyes widened and a big smile lit up her face.

I took one more breath as it rang again and then, calmly, I answered. "Well, if it's not the elusive Mr. E. Hello."

"Hello, gorgeous."

Edward's voice sent a shiver down my spine. Damn. I had it bad.

"I know this is last minute, but do you have plans this weekend? I got a lot done at work the past few days in the hopes I could take you out of the city."

I locked myself in the bathroom so I could have some privacy and used the time to pretend to check the calendar on my phone. Not that I needed to check it—what would I put on it? Work? Period due? Work?

I quickly calculated all of the assignments my boss had given me before I answered, "I have a couple of deadlines to finish before Friday, but I think I can work it out. What did you have in mind?"

"I know a quaint little lodge in the Catskills. How do you feel about hiking?"

"Sore," I said. "My legs already feel sore. I'm more a city sidewalks girl and I don't remember the last time I climbed a hill."

He laughed. "Well, luckily our room has a hot tub on the deck."

I didn't even hesitate. "Count me in."

We hung up shortly after that and I sighed,

clutching the phone to my chest and not even bothering to pretend I wasn't relieved.

***

Late Friday afternoon, Edward picked me up in a silver BMW and I tried not to let my jaw drop. I don't know why it surprised me. It would've been crazy to make Paul drive all that way, drop us off and drive back to the city.

And having him there would be awkward, I thought, still eying his gorgeous car.

"You're driving? What will Paul say? Is he heartbroken?" I teased.

Edward winked at me. "I wanted you all to myself this weekend. Paul will get over it."

He stowed my bag and we climbed in, the nerves already chattering inside me. We had a long drive and my head was already churning. I had the worst habit of blurting things out at the worst possible time. Things like...*so, why won't you tell me who you are?* I wasn't sure I could avoid it for the hours we'd be trapped in the car.

It came as a relief when he broached the subject first.

"I want to apologize for my reluctance to talk about my family." He glanced at me. "And for not giving you my last name. My family name is, ah, recognizable and I just want to know that you're with me, not my name."

112

Relief washed over me. That made sense. He was rich, which would already make him wary of the reasons why someone would want to be with him.

A well-known family name had to make it worse.

"Bad experiences?" I asked, hearing something in his voice.

He hesitated and then nodded. "One or two. I'm..." He blew out a slow, careful breath. "I try not to let it color my life, but I told myself I was going to make sure somebody cared about me the next time. I hope you understand."

My heart ached and I found myself smiling. "I do. And thank you."

"Why are you thanking me?"

I leaned over and kissed him on the cheek. "Because you trusted me enough to tell me. I love that you felt comfortable enough to tell me that."

He caught my hand and lifted it to his lips, pressing a kiss to the back of it. When he pressed it to his thigh before putting his hand back on the wheel, I let myself breathe out a sigh of satisfaction.

"I do understand," I said again. "But, just so you know..." When he flicked a look at me, I winked. "I want you to know that I'm with you, not your name, no matter what it is." I squeezed his thigh and felt his muscles tighten. "And now we can relax."

"No," he said, pulling the car into a wooded turn out. "Not yet."

The car was still shuddering from the speed with which he'd thrown it into park when he pulled me over the center console and sideways onto his lap. I bumped my head against his window, but didn't care as he caught me in a searing kiss. His lips were hard and insistent against mine. Almost immediately, I was glad I'd dismissed Kendra's advice and worn a dress because Edward's hand quickly found the hem and slid underneath.

His mouth ate at mine, his tongue thrusting deep into my mouth as his palm slid up my thigh, pushing my skirt up. He cupped my hip and I felt the heat of his arousal burning against my skin. My own desire started to rise inside me and I whimpered hungrily, catching his tongue and sucking on it.

He shuddered and shifted me until I was straddling him, his fingers tracing me through my panties. "You're already wet for me. Did you miss me?"

"Yes." My eyelids fluttered as he rubbed slow teasing circles around my clitoris, working with the material to create a delicious friction that had me moaning and writhing against his hand. He chuckled as he moved his hand up to my stomach and then slipped it down into my panties. Two fingers spread my folds apart as his middle finger slid inside.

"Fuck," I whimpered. Wanting more, I put my knee up on the console, trying to open myself more completely.

A second finger thrust deep and I cried out. His mouth sucked on the place where my shoulder and neck met, teeth scraping over the soft skin as he worked his fingers in and out with a relentless rhythm, not stopping until I shuddered and came against his hand.

I was still trembling when he turned me so that I was leaning forward over the steering wheel, one leg on either side of his lap. I lifted up on shaky knees as he reached beneath me and unzipped his pants. I was glad we'd covered the condom thing before because there was no pause as he grasped my hips and pulled me down onto him.

He swore as he filled me, his arms wrapping around my waist to hold me in place.

"So tight," he said, his voice muffled as he pressed his face against my back. "I've been wanting you so badly. I don't know how long I can last."

"Don't then," I said. My body was still tingling from my orgasm and the feel of him throbbing inside me was enough to start the pressure building again. I moved one hand under my dress. It wasn't going to take much to get me off again.

"Are you sure?"

I nodded.

He gripped my hips and lifted me enough so he could move. My head brushed the ceiling and I leaned forward more as my fingers made their way to the place where our bodies joined.

There was so little room to move. He didn't *thrust* within me—it was more like a hard, deep grinding that had me shuddering, shaking deep inside, pleasure jolting through me hard and fast as I manipulated my clit.

His cock pulsed and throbbed and I heard him mutter my name. I stroked myself harder, faster. His cock jerked and I arched, my climax slamming into me just as he started to come.

I slumped forward, my body quaking with its release.

His arms tightened around my waist as he pulled me back against him. I rested my head on his shoulder, enjoying the feel of him holding me, of our bodies still intimately joined.

He kissed my cheek. "Now we can relax."

***

My breath was taken away as soon as I opened my eyes the next morning. We'd arrived rumpled sometime after sunset and I'd been so tired, I'd collapsed not long after a light dinner.

Now, with Edward kneeling next to the bed with a mimosa and a devilish smile, it was hard to take everything in. Through the window behind him, I could see the river valley and tumbling green hills stretched out endlessly. The view alone was staggering, but I was here with him.

I couldn't imagine anything more perfect.

"Good morning, gorgeous," he said. "Sorry if I woke you. Are you hungry?"

"Hmmm." I looked back out the window and then at him. "Are we really hiking?" I'd do it for him, but I wasn't exactly looking forward to it.

"Well." He gave me a sly smile that said he

already knew what my answer would be. "There's also a couples spa package, if you would prefer."

***

After breakfast in bed, we surrendered our day to the capable hands of the spa staff. Or, at least, I did. Edward had no interest in pedicures by the pool, so he swam laps while I enjoyed one, and a massage. I wanted to close my eyes at the heavenly pressure of the foot rub, but I couldn't tear my eyes away from him.

Even wet, there were streaks of gold coming out in his light brown hair. His hands and neck were slightly darker due to his days out on the polo fields, but he looked golden.

I watched him, strong and lithe in the pool, not only because he was gorgeous, but because it was easier than taking in our surroundings. I'd never been in a hotel so luxurious and I felt out of place. I was sure the woman scrubbing at my neglected feet was shaking her head at the thought of another rich man dragging some pretty girl up from the gutter.

Could we ever really fit?

He was from a family with pedigree, a public image, and a clearly healthy empire. I was a country girl trying to make it in the big city, just barely scraping by day to day.

What exactly did he see in me?

When the spa attendant finished packing us into

our mud baths and left us alone in the steamy Turkish tiled room, I had to blink back tears. Even here, the luxury followed us, reminding me of who he was versus who I was.

"Is yours too hot? Want me to ring for the attendant?" His voice was soft, tender with concern.

I shook my head. "No, no, that's not it." My throat tightened up. "I just don't think I can handle all of this."

"The pampering?" he asked, clearly confused.

"No," I said. I couldn't keep it inside anymore. "Edward, I'm out of place here. If it wasn't for you, I'd never be able to afford so much as a glass of mineral water for the bar here. Doesn't it bother you?"

Mud squelched as he sat up, but he ignored it. Face somber, he gazed at me. "Listen to me. I'm paying because I want you here with me. I don't expect you to pay for any of this. I probably wouldn't be able to either if it wasn't for my family."

"But you run their big company doing whatever it is you do," I said.

"And you write and get coffee." He laughed softly and reached out, trailing a hand down my mud-slicked arm. "I'm surprised you haven't been pulled into modeling. Kendra's one of the big up and comers and you're so beautiful. I'm sure somebody has seen you, noticed you..."

My stomach dropped.

"I did," I said slowly.

"Oh?" His brows shot up.

"I did a shoot. Once. I was never called back."

"Sounds like it didn't go well." Concern darkened his eyes.

The sight of it had my belly twisted. "It's not that. I just..."

"Tell me you didn't end up with one of those slimy photographers who seduces every woman he gets in front of the camera," he said, disgust thick in his voice.

And that clinched it. Shame a hot, heavy weight in me, I lied. "No. It just wasn't my thing. When he didn't call me back in, I was relieved."

"It's not for everybody." Edward caught my hand and squeezed, swinging back onto the table. "I'm glad you're here with me, Gabriella. I *want* you here with me."

Face burning, I closed my eyes.

Between the guilt from the lie and the annoying sense that I wasn't doing anything to earn what I had going on, it was almost impossible to relax, but slowly, bit by bit, I did. Succumbing to the heat of the bath, the tension gave way and the guilt that sat like a stone in my belly began to dissolve.

I hadn't intended to sleep with Flynn.

I'd thought I'd sensed something with him, something real. But I hadn't. Maybe he was one of those sleazy photographers. I'd put it behind me. There was no reason for it to cloud things between Edward and me and it wasn't like it was going to ever haunt me again. I hadn't even signed a release for the pictures, so he couldn't use them.

Photographers had to have a release—that was one thing I knew from working with Kendra. I had taken the money though.

As to the opulence of the lodge, and everything else that came from being with Edward...that was just as complicated.

Mentally groaning over the frustration, I told myself to let it go.

You're not trying to get anything out of him, Gabs. It's not like you've ever asked for anything from him.

Finally, the logic pierced me and the misery began to sink away. I hadn't asked for him to treat me to these extravagances. I didn't expect them. I was still working and struggling and paying my own way in life.

I just needed to relax and enjoy what he was giving me...right?

But still, the uneasiness lingered.

So did the weight of the lie. Even if I tried to pretend otherwise.

***

By the time we were done, both Edward and I were happy rag-dolls and I'd all but forgotten about the awkward exchange. As we headed back to our room, Flynn and the photo shoot were the furthest things from my mind. Edward was the most caring, considerate, and generous lover I had ever been with and I wanted to spend my time making him feel how much I appreciated him, not thinking about past mistakes.

As he lay on the bed, loose in a plush hotel robe, I dropped mine to the floor and slowly crawled up next to him. When I saw his sleepy grin, I gave him a long, thorough kiss before trailing my lips down his jaw to nuzzle underneath his ear.

The faint scent of lavender and bergamot was still on his skin from the massage oil and I tasted him with my tongue before trailing kisses down his chest. I could feel his heart thumping wildly as I pressed my mouth over it. His robe parted easily and my breasts brushed against his erection as I slid down his body, a singular destination in mind.

He was already starting to harden, but still soft enough that I could take all of him. He smothered a cry when I took him between my lips and a thrill went through me. I loved knowing I could make him feel this way, make his cock stiffen and grow.

I held him as long as I could before he was too big and I had to settle for wrapping my hand around the base of him while I began to move my head up and down. The thick vein pulsed against my tongue and he started to move against my mouth, until I pressed down on his hipbones with my hands.

"Be still," I said, lifting my head to smile at him.

"Witch." He groaned, dropping his head back onto the pillow.

I slid my lips up, then down his length, loving the way the caress made him shudder. His hands fisted in the elegant brocade of the comforter below him. A raw noise left his throat as I sucked on him, taking him all the way to the back of my throat before changing to softer, slow licks up and down his cock.

His hands left the comforter to grip my shoulders, tugging on me and I lifted my head to smile at him.

"Dammit, Gabriella."

Coming to my knees, I crawled up his body and hovered over him. I was so wet, so ready for him. The inside of my thighs were slick with my need as I straddled him. Edward gripped my waist, staring at me with hooded, hungry eyes. I caught his cock, still wet from my mouth and held him as I began to lower myself down.

He slid his hands up, cupping my breasts, plumping them together as his cock stretched me wide. The sensation was almost too much, too fast, and my legs trembled. Then he was fully sheathed inside me and I sighed at the way our bodies came together. I didn't stay still long though. His head arched off the pillow as I began to ride him.

His hands left my breasts to grip my hips, fingers digging into my flesh, his mouth open in soundless ecstasy. I felt him swell inside me and I cried out because it was too much. The head of his cock rubbed against my g-spot, sending waves of heat arcing through me. Edward started to arch up off the bed, rising to meet me until we were driving into his each other.

The intensity of it overwhelmed me. I went flying into orgasm and I thought I was spinning, flying—then I realized Edward had flipped me over, planting me under him. He slammed into me and I cried out again. Harder, harder...he sent me into another climax just as he began to come.

My body ached in the most delicious way and I wouldn't have traded it for anything.

***

When I came out of my shower more than an hour later, Edward wasn't there, but I did find a luscious blue satin dress laid out on the bed. A thin black velvet box sat next to it and on the floor were a delicate pair of designer shoes. A note on the hotel's stationary was propped up like a sign:

The gifts I give you are nothing compared to your beauty, your time, and your love. All of which I want always. –Edward

My heart soared. All of my doubts and suspicions were erased with those words and I dressed in a whirl of fairytale thoughts.

Chapter Nine

The Catskills lodge was old-fashioned, with a two-story curving staircase leading down to a chandelier-lit foyer. As per instructions I received via text, I went down on my own. I was practically floating as I came down the stairs and found Edward waiting at the bottom with a single white rose.

He held it out to me. "You look like a dream come true."

I touched the delicate sapphire and diamond necklace, tears stinging my eyes. I'd never had anyone treat me this way before. "Thank you."

He leaned down and kissed me softly, a bare brush of lips but the contact was enough to send a rush of heat through me. He straightened, looked down at me for a moment, then tucked my hand in the crook of his elbow and led me down a candlelit corridor to the back porch.

The wide porch ran the entire back of the hotel and offered a seemingly endless choice of white sofas, softly cushioned rattan armchairs, and swings. The whole expanse was lit by hurricane lamps and lanterns casting a soft glow on the other guests enjoying a drink before dinner.

Edward and I each took a glass of champagne from a passing waiter before he took me down the stairs and onto a path winding through the great lawn. It swept gracefully away from the lodge and out to a breathtaking view of the Hudson River Valley. The sun was just past setting, the sky bleeding to a deep velvet glow. It would gradually give way to the inky darkness of night. Away from the soft lights of the porch, stars already twinkled in the cloudless sky.

"I don't think this night could be any more perfect." I sighed.

He clinked his champagne flute against mine and we paused to sip and stare up at the diamond glitter overhead. The silence between us was thick with tension, but it was a pleasant kind, the kind that promised something more to follow.

"I meant what I said in my note." Edward broke the silence.

I kissed his cheek, not trusting myself to try anything chaste enough for public. "Always," I said.

"I was hoping you'd say that." He walked me along a narrow stone path down to the rose garden where a stone fountain splashed gently. The underwater lights made the water shimmer. In the undulating glow, he caught my eyes and held my gaze.

He brushed back a few strands of hair as he spoke, "I've never felt this way about any other woman. The time I spend with you is truly the best part of my life."

Suddenly, he went down on one knee and caught my hands before I could smother my cry of surprise. This couldn't be happening. It couldn't be real.

"Gabriella, would you do the great honor of marrying me?"

The night sky spun above me and I hung on to Edward's hands to keep myself grounded. I knew if I let go, I wouldn't even be able to stand.

"Are you—are you serious?" My eyes were wide, heart racing.

He looked up at me with a pained smile. Clearly, that was not the reaction he'd been expecting.

"Yes!" He rolled his eyes. "How can I convince you?"

I let go of his hands and cupped his face before leaning down to kiss him. It was short but fierce. "Like this." His eyes were shining as he looked up at me. "Yes, Edward. Yes, I'll marry you!"

***

It was a little past three in the morning when I sat bolt upright in a cold sweat. The heavy diamond engagement ring winked at me in the dim room and I stared at it as my heart pounded. It was unreal, the flawless emerald cut diamond flashing at me like a star in the night. What had seemed like a fairytale dream now felt like the start of a nightmare.

"What's the matter?" Edward asked sleepily as

my sudden movement woke him.

"What if we're rushing this?" My doubts came pouring out. There were a hundred of them and I couldn't even begin to list them all. As he sat there staring at me, befuddled, I raked a hand through my hair.

I still didn't know his last name.

I didn't know what he did for a living.

His family...oh, shit.

Clambering out of bed, I grabbed the robe that had been draped over a nearby chair. Shoving my arms into it, I started to pace. The doubts grew larger and larger and I could feel Edward watching me, feel his concern and his care. Turning, I stared at him.

"I haven't even met your family, Edward. What if they meet me and hate me? They'll convince you this was a huge mistake. *You'll* think I'm a huge mistake."

He pushed himself up on his elbows. His hair was mussed, making him look younger than usual. His expression was serious. "I'll never think that."

I shook my head. "You're already under enough pressure from them, running the family empire. I'm just going to make things worse for you."

"Only if you don't let me sleep." His voice held a teasing note as he sat up. He held out his hand and I went to him. He pulled me into his lap and I sat down. He tucked his chin into my shoulder and held me close, my body pressed to his.

When we were like this, any and all doubt faded.

I felt certain. I felt safe and loved and right. But...

"They'll think I'm a gold-digger," I continued. "How could they not? I don't bring anything to the table. I don't even know what table I'm bringing it to."

"Gabriella, we're adults." He brushed my hair away from my neck. "I'm an adult and I'm not going to let my family tell me who I can love. I love you." His voice softened. "Don't you believe me?"

"I do," I said. "I want to believe you."

"I understand." His hands fell away from my shoulders.

Shit. I'd hurt his feelings. I turned towards him, needing him to understand. "I believe you. I love you. I do. I'm just scared. This feels like a dream."

His voice was soft as he reached for my hands. "What can I do to make you understand this is real, that we are really getting married and that I'm thrilled you said yes?"

I knew what I was going to say would hurt him, but I couldn't lie about it, not if we were going to have a life together. "It won't feel real, won't feel possible, until I meet your family. I'm sorry, Edward, but I don't think I can marry you until I know the family I will be marrying into." The one thing I didn't add was that I also needed to see for myself how he'd behave when his parents discovered where I came from.

He flopped back on the pillows and heaved a big sigh. I'd known he wasn't going to like what I had to say. But could he blame me?

I picked up his arm and wrapped it around my shoulder, pulling it tight as I stretched out next to him, putting my head on his chest. For several minutes, neither of us spoke. I listened to his heartbeat and tried to ignore the sound of his teeth grinding.

I needed him to understand. "This is going to be for the rest of our lives, Edward. Always. I can't go into that thinking your family wishes it wasn't me."

He didn't say anything, but he kissed my head as his fingers made slow circles on my upper arm. It was comforting, but not enough. Minutes ticked by and I tried not to cry. Whatever happened now was going to decide if I got my happily ever after or not. The pure reflection of the perfect emerald cut diamond caught the slim moonlight from the window and I tipped it back and forth, wondering how long I'd be wearing it.

"This is ridiculous," Edward finally said.

He slipped out from under me and sat up. Before I could stop him, he tossed the covers aside and slapped his bare feet onto the floor. I watched his lean muscles ripple as he strode across the room naked. As hot as he was, I couldn't focus on that.

"What are you doing?" I asked, hating the way my voice shook.

"Calling my mother."

I stared at him. "But it's past three in the morning!"

"This is exciting news and it can't wait," he said as he dialed.

I held my breath as I listened to his half of the phone conversation.

"Mother, it's Edward. No, everything's fine." He paused for a moment and then continued, "Yes, I got your notes on the spring line. Mother, I have exciting news. I asked Gabriella to marry me and she said yes."

There was a long pause and I could feel my chest tightening as I waited.

"That's exactly what she said," he sounded amused. "Yes, perfect. Gabriella and I will meet you and Father tomorrow at the club. Thank you. Goodnight. Yes, right, good morning."

He padded back across the room and dove into the bed, wrapping his arms around me. He pulled me close, pressing his mouth against my ear. "Now come here and tell me your answer again."

"Yes," I said with a smile. "Yes, I will marry you."

***

Back to reality...or maybe not.

Instead of sleeping in and waking with slow, leisurely sex, followed by a slow, leisurely breakfast, we were up by seven, on the road by eight and back into the city about the same time I would have preferred to have been rolling out of bed.

We went by the apartment I shared with Kendra, my nerves singing as I opened the door. But she wasn't there and I was spared the tension of telling her what should have been happy news.

I was dreading her reaction. I thought she'd be happy for me, but still, Edward and I had only been dating a few weeks. It felt right, but even I knew this was fast and until I met his family, I'd have misgivings.

Kendra would sense those and I didn't want that.

I wanted to be certain when I faced her.

She'd understand it better if I was certain.

She'd know if I wasn't.

I hurriedly grabbed some clothes. Edward had convinced me to get ready at his place, so I just traded out the outfit I'd planned to wear for the clothes I'd packed for the lodge. I still had my toiletries. It took less than ten minutes and we were back on the road.

The drive to his place was silent.

It wasn't uncomfortable, but it was unsettling. Once we reached the staggering stone mansion, my nerves returned in triplicate. The home was impressive and now I was seeing it in a whole new light.

Soon, I would be part of this legacy.

The house was grand, but I had only ever felt comfortable in Edward's master suite or the study. The other rooms, the glimpses I'd gotten of them anyway, seemed hollow.

I buried myself in his bathroom. He'd offered to use one of the others and I was too grateful to argue.

Now, as I blow-dried my hair, studied my reflection, applied my make-up only to wash it off and start again, I couldn't fight the rising tide of nerves.

Edward appeared in the mirror behind me, already dressed in a suit that cost more than I made in a month, naked pictures included. I gulped.

"You look terrified." Resting his hands on my shoulders, he pressed a kiss to my shoulder, bare save for the strap of my camisole. "Relax."

"I can't!" Panicked, I stared at my reflection. Simple, ordinary me, lost in the elegance of his white and gold bathroom. "We're getting ready to meet your family. I feel so out of place."

"First, we've got time. Second, you're *not* out of place. You're with me, right where I want you to be." He slid a hand up and cupped my cheek, guiding my head back against his shoulder. "And I'm with you. Where you want me to be, right?"

The calm assurance of his voice did something to level me.

Taking a deep, slow breath, I forced myself to nod. "Yes."

"Good." He turned me around and his mouth closed over mine in a deep, slow kiss.

"Hmmm..."

He pressed his brow to mine and for a moment, we stood there like that. Then he lifted his head. "I've a few more calls to make. Why don't you spend some time walking around, seeing more of the house? You hardly ever go outside my..." Then he grinned, the smile bright and open. "Soon it will be *our* room. At least until we find a place to make *ours*. But walk around the house. Get to know it better. Alright?"

***

I found Paul in what looked like the kitchen of a first class restaurant. He was chatting with a cute redhead, but when they saw me, it was like they both jerked to attention.

"Miss Gabriella." Paul smiled warmly. "Do you need something? Are you lost?"

I winced. "Maybe." Then, because kitchens, at least, were something I understood, I eased farther inside. "Edward said he had to get some work done before we left and I..." I shrugged. "I wanted to look around."

They stood by while I wandered the kitchen and then Paul came to my side. "Why don't I show you around, Miss Gabriella?"

Feeling more and more like an intruder, I nodded. The redhead looked nervous and I tried to give her a friendly smile, but she wouldn't look at me.

As we left the kitchen, she busied herself at the counter. Once the door swung shut behind us, I blew out a breath. "Did I mess up?"

"Of course not." Paul gave me a polite smile.

He'd say that even if I'd broken every dish in the place.

"You've worked for Edward a long time, haven't you?"

"I have." He glanced down a hall and then at me. "Do you enjoy gardens? There's a greenhouse with lovely flowers. They bloom all year."

"Sure." Anything was fine as long as I wasn't thinking—or lost. "Do you like your job?"

"Very much." There was no doubting his sincerity.

"So how long have you worked for Edward?" I couldn't believe I hadn't thought to ask him before.

"I've been with his family for twelve years now."

"What are they like?" I asked.

Paul smiled, but it was tight-lipped and he said nothing. Apparently that was a line I couldn't cross.

"Please." I spread out of my hands to encompass everybody in the house—the servants who were mostly invisible, the redhead I had somehow made nervous, Edward, Paul. "None of ya'll have any idea how nervous I'm getting over the idea of meeting his parents." I groaned. "And look there. My Tennessee is showing."

The crack made Paul chuckle and he sighed. After a moment, he relented. "They can be very stiff, very snobbish. They can be very set in their ways, but you must understand, they do love him. Edward's mother would do anything for him. She wants what's best for him."

"And his father?"

Paul shook his head, like he'd said too much, but I didn't give up.

"What about his siblings? Edward said everyone would be there today." I stopped in the middle of the path and looked around, realizing we were in the middle of the greenhouse. I hadn't even noticed. The heat started to sink into my bones and I felt lightheaded, although it wasn't from the temperature. "I think I'm going to faint."

Taking pity on me, he guided me over to a curved, wide bench. "His brothers are different; a little, ah, freer. They don't have the same responsibilities as Edward. He's the eldest son and he has a specific role to play in his family. He's a good man, Miss. Gabriella."

I agreed with that. "He's the best man I've ever met."

As if that was his cue, the doors to the greenhouse swung open and Edward came striding in. "I was hoping you would think to show her the greenhouse. I swung by the kitchen looking for you, Gabriella. Hayley said Paul was giving you a tour."

I smiled at him, determined not to let him see my nerves.

Cut straight from a high-priced catalog in perfectly pressed khakis, a white polo shirt, and a blue sports coat, he came toward me, so elegant and perfect...and mine. Paul quietly excused himself and I rose to meet Edward. I smoothed a hand down my linen dress.

"You look lovely," Edward said, catching my hand and lifting it to his lips.

"Do I?" I glanced down at my dress. "The

color...does it clash with my hair?"

He bent his head and kissed me. "You're lovely," he reiterated. He slid his hands up and down my arms. "You're tense. What's wrong?"

"I'm terrified." Slowly, I lifted my eyes to his and shrugged. "Your family...I mean, you've said you've had a couple of rough relationships. What if they think I'm just some gold digger and they try to scare me away?"

"What if they do?" he countered. "Will you let them?"

I looked up at him and his eyes searched my face. He was honestly concerned and that chased away some of my own fear. I kissed his cheek and then scrubbed off the lipstick smudge.

"No," I said firmly. "But what if my accent slips or I get mad and call them snobs?"

"Then we'll laugh and they'll get over it."

***

As Paul drove, Edward kept me distracted with clever comments about people he'd met at various events at the club. I mentioned some of the plaids I'd seen men wearing on golf tournaments on TV which brought up a whole new conversation.

I ended up laughing away some of the tension, but as we pulled up to the security gate, an offhand comment he made brought up a whole new set of concerns.

"I'll have you added to my membership," he said, catching my hand and squeezing it. "I rarely come here, but you might enjoy it. Once you're my wife, you might find yourself with more free time on your hands."

Free time...?

I went to ask him what that meant, but the gates opened up and he nodded ahead. "It's time, love."

Free time.

Time.

Shit. We hadn't talked about what things would be like when we were married. We hadn't discussed my writing, my job. Did he want me to quit the job I hated? Yeah, he could support me, but I didn't want to become one of those women who lived off of her husband. And what about kids? Did he want them?

Did *I*?

All of those questions and more were on the tip of my tongue.

But the car stopped.

A moment later, Paul was opening the door for us.

Time was up.

Chapter Ten

Mouth dry, pulse racing, I took Edward's arm and he steered me through the formal dining room and out onto a sun-drenched patio that overlooked a carefully pruned garden.

"A mimosa and a screwdriver, light on the orange juice," he told a passing waiter. He looked down at me, "Is that all right?"

I shrugged, not trusting myself to speak. What I really wanted though was whiskey. A double.

I felt like I had a million eyes staring at me and if an alarm had started blaring *INTRUDER ALERT, INTRUDER ALERT,* I wouldn't have been surprised.

Were people staring?

Was it that obvious I didn't belong?

"Are you okay?" Edward's voice low, so low I barely heard him.

I nodded. Off to the corner, a group of women, probably in their fifties or so, glanced our way. One of them eyed me, from the top of my head down to my shoes. Her nostrils flared as she sniffed and I felt the red rush to my cheeks.

Men were gathered in a group close by.

I didn't see any couples together. Everybody was grouped together by gender. And Edward thought I'd hang out here? Who would I talk to? The people bringing out the drinks? I'd certainly feel a lot more comfortable with them.

"Is that what we'll be like?" I asked suddenly. I gestured towards the groups. "Doing our own thing, you discussing business with the men while I'm off with the women talking about parties and raising the kids?"

His mouth twitched in amusement. "I hope not. I don't want separate but connected lives. I want our life, Gabriella." He leaned in, brushed a kiss over my cheek. "You can have a career or do as my mother did, get involved in charities...or raise the kids." He gave me a mischievous smile. "You decide. One thing though. I'm not changing my name to Baine. But if you don't want to change yours, that's fine too."

While I was still nervous, I did feel a measure of relief at his words. Now I just had to keep myself distracted until it was time to meet the future in-laws.

"That reminds me, I'm about to find out your family name. Does that mean you're going to turn into a pumpkin? Or is it more of a Rumpelstiltskin thing where you'll have to grant me a wish?"

Edward laughed and I felt myself relax even more. I could do this as long as he was with me.

"I'll grant you a wish for every day that you're mine," he said.

"Well, my first wish is for one of those heavenly croissants. I'm starving."

I watched a basket of the buttery pastries bob by on a waiter's tray, but before I could snag one, the hostess came by.

"Mr. Edward? Your party is here."

We walked arm in arm into the formal dining room. In the doorway, we paused a moment and I had that split second to try and guess who Edward's parents were.

A half dozen couples could have been contenders. Several tall, distinguished men, several attractive women with brown hair. But nobody stuck out and then time was up, because Edward was already guiding me to a table occupied by a handsome man who appeared to be in his fifties, still robust and powerful looking. The woman was blonde and statuesque. The moment she looked up, I could see where Edward had gotten his ice blue eyes.

She stood, eyes only for her son. "Edward, darling, it's been too long."

Edward kissed her cheek and then nodded at the man I assumed was his father even though they didn't look anything alike. "Mother, this is Gabriella. Gabriella, this is my mother, Claire."

Claire shook my hand lightly and I could tell she thought about reaching for a napkin when I let go.

"And now I see what's been keeping you away." Her expression was tight.

Edward pulled out her chair and waited until

she sat down to kiss her on the cheek again. She patted his cheek and then waved me to the chair next to her. I sat down without assistance and was glad to catch Edward's wink as he circled the table to sit next to me.

"What a lovely necklace, Claire. May I call you Claire?" I asked.

Claire gave a faint smile and flagged down a waiter without answering my question. "We'll need one more place setting, please. The three of you are always busy, but at least one of your brothers is able to join us, I hear."

"I know. He texted me earlier. The more the merrier." Edward smiled. "It'll be nice for her to meet more of the family."

"So, Gabriella, what do you do for a living?" Mr. Rumpelstiltskin or whatever their last name was gave me a pleasant smile.

"I'm an assistant for a writer for a television show, but I'm hoping to write my own someday." I braced myself for the usual onslaught of comments that followed a pronouncement of a career in the arts.

"So you're hoping to use Edward's name to further your own career...?"

I interrupted before Edward was forced to say something to his mother that would make her hate me even more. "Actually, Claire, Edward hasn't told me much about your family, only that he's involved in the family business. My interest in him is purely him."

"She makes it sound like we run a mom and pop shop." Claire sipped a glass of champagne then dabbed her lips with a white linen napkin.

"Did he take over for you?" I asked the much more friendly face across from me.

"Me?" He looked surprised. "No. I'm actually Edward's stepfather. You can call me Albert."

"I'm so sorry! How rude of me," Edward said. "Albert and my mother have been married for eons. I can't believe I didn't introduce you two."

Albert smiled and waved a hand, like he was used to being forgotten. "Why don't you tell us about the marriage proposal before you tire of telling the story?"

Edward pulled our joined hands up above the white tablecloth and held up my engagement ring. He squeezed my fingers. "Starlight, champagne, a fountain in the rose garden. I must have done it right because this beauty said 'yes'."

Claire shot my emerald cut diamond solitaire a begrudgingly impressed look.

"How did you and Albert meet?" I asked, determined to win her over.

"Albert was the headmaster at the boarding school I wished for my boys to attend. They were still young, of course, but one must be diligent if one wants only the best for their children." She looked over at her husband. "Of course, once we decided to get married, he had to resign so as to avoid the appearance of favoritism."

I decided to go with a question that had nothing

to do with how odd I thought it was that her husband had to give up his job rather than just sending the kids to another school. "You went to an all-boys boarding school?" I asked Edward.

"One of the finest in the country," Claire said it like there was no other option. "Where were you educated?"

Her attitude sucked. Arching a brow, I smiled coolly. "Tennessee public schools."

Her gaze slid to Edward's. He stared back, his face impassive. After a moment, she smiled a little and began to discuss work.

It took less than a minute to figure out that they were involved in the fashion industry. It took less than five to realize that they just might have a fair hand in controlling it. My heart started to race and under the table, I twisted my hands over and over around the heavy material of the napkin I'd put in my lap.

Kendra had told me about the executives who could make or break entire collections and countless careers with one phone call. That probably explained why she thought she recognized him, but couldn't put a name to a face.

The sommelier brought champagne to the table. "Here you are, Mrs. Bouvier."

My jaw dropped. "I'm sorry, did you just say Bouvier?"

*Bouvier...shit. Edward...Bouvier...*my heart was about to jump out of my chest. Lifting my gaze, I stared at him. "I...you..." Shaking my head, I looked around and then said, "Are y'all seriously the *Bouviers*?"

I heard the accent thickening my voice, but I couldn't even think about that now.

From the corner of my eye, I could see his mother watching me, could see the sommelier fighting not to do the same.

Edward laughed, a sheepish smile on his face. "I told you my last name was quite recognizable."

"You didn't tell her your last name?" Claire raised an eyebrow.

Edward's expression stiffened. "I thought you'd be pleased, Mother. We dated, fell in love, and she agreed to marry me all without knowing I'm a Bouvier."

"I don't believe this," I said, pressing my hand to my forehead.

"Gabriella, are you well?"

The soft question came from the man across from me.

Weakly, I looked at him. "I'm fine, Mr. Bouvier—"

"Albert is *not* Mr. Bouvier. His name is Albert McCreary," Claire said, her voice pure ice. She stared at me, clearly offended. "When I remarried, I kept my first married name because of the company and my sons."

I barely heard the final words she said, though...

Coincidence?

Had to be.

McCreary...

No way.

"Hey there, big brother. I hear I'm getting a sister-in-law..."

The familiar voice trailed off as I lifted my head.

He moved around the table, all sexy grace and cadet blue eyes. My future brother-in-law. Flynn McCreary.

Shit.

Acknowledgement

First, we would like to thank all of our readers. Without you, our books would not exist. We truly appreciate each and every one of you.

A big "thanks" goes out to all the Facebook fans, street team, beta readers, and advanced reviewers. You are a HUGE part of the success of the series.

We have to thank our PA, Shannon Hunt. Without you our lives would be a complete and utter mess. Also a big thank you goes out to our editor Lynette and our wonderful cover designer, Sinisa. You make our ideas and writing look so good.

About The Authors

MS Parker

M. S. Parker is a USA Today Bestselling author and the author of the Erotic Romance series, Club Privè and Chasing Perfection.

Living in Southern California, she enjoys sitting by the pool with her laptop writing on her next spicy romance.

Growing up all she wanted to be was a dancer, actor or author. So far only the latter has come true but M. S. Parker hasn't retired her dancing shoes just yet. She is still waiting for the call for her to appear on Dancing With The Stars.

When M. S. isn't writing, she can usually be found reading– oops, scratch that! She is always writing.

Cassie Wild

Cassie Wild loves romance. Every since she was eight years old she's been reading every romance novel she could get her hands on, always dreaming of writing her own romance novels.

When MS Parker approached her about co-authoring the Serving HIM series, it didn't take Cassie many seconds to say a big yes!!

Serving HIM is only the beginning to the collaboration between MS Parker and Cassie Wild. Another series is already in the planning stages.

Made in the USA
San Bernardino, CA
08 July 2015